Twitter: @LEckhart
Facebook: AuthorLorhainneEckhart

Printed in the U.S.A

PLAY HARD TO GET

The Parker Sisters

LORHAINNE ECKHART

The Parker Sisters

The Parker Sisters, a spinoff of the romance series Married in Montana from a Readers' Favorite award-winning author and "queen of the family saga" (Aherman)

The Parker Sisters
Thrill of the Chase
The Dating Game
Play Hard to Get
What We Can't Have
Go Your Own Way
A June Wedding

Thrill of the Chase: A small-town country girl who works as an EMT. An accidental bystander who falls hard for her. Will her complicated family life ruin their budding romance?

The Dating Game: A sexy single nurse looking for love.

Two handsome, eligible men quickly step up, but one of them is a total mystery. Can she solve the puzzle and figure out which one is Mr. Right?

Playing Hard to Get: A journalist chasing a big story. The corrupt, powerful subject she's out to expose. But what if the truth about him turns her life upside down?

What We Can't Have: Love triangles can be complicated…especially when the heartthrob is a rodeo hero and two sisters end up vying to capture his heart!

Go Your Own Way: An untamed beauty with plans for a life beyond the family ranch. A dashing stranger who's beholden to no one. Will the sparks between them lead to true love?

A June Wedding: Dearly beloved, we are gathered in this month of June for a wedding at the Parker family ranch. Or so the invitation says! Little does the family know that not just one Parker sister is getting married, but three. Will this be the wedding of the season, or will three sisters end up with broken hearts?

A journalist chasing a big story. The corrupt, powerful subject she's out to expose. But what if the truth about him turns her life upside down?

Chapter One

Staring at her unfamiliar image in the mirror was both exciting and shocking. Naomi Parker had never been blond, sultry, a walking sex kitten—and without glasses. But that was in fact the image before her now. It gave her a thrill. She was living on the edge, becoming someone she was born to be deep down, playing a part that was dangerous but would solidify Naomi for who she really was, a rockstar journalist who would uncover anything and everything that no one else could.

Just as quickly as the thought excited her, it worried her, because unfortunately her parents, Robert and Susan, and her sisters had no idea what she'd gotten herself into. If they found out this side of her that she hid from everyone, well, let's just say she hated to think what their response would be—after the shock wore off, that is. Something close to "Over my dead body" or "Hell no," with a dash of "What were you thinking?" and, to finish it off, "How do we get her out of this mess so she'll again be the daughter we raised her to be?"

To Naomi, though, it wasn't a mess or a pending disaster. She was chasing the story of a lifetime, a story no one else would touch, about a man with a sordid past. A monster, according to the people of Casper, Wyoming, with his bad attitude, dangerous good looks, linebacker build, and eyes that could stop a woman cold. Not that she knew what that meant, but Naomi had every intention of exposing Cameron Donnelly for the lying, cheating fraud he was, for an abuser of power who'd dominated the local headlines just one year earlier. He was all everyone could talk about and had become the man you didn't want to be associated with.

How she was going to do that was still forming in her mind, but she could feel the sizzle of this new Naomi—oops, or rather, Julie, with her bleached hair, colored contact lenses making her blue eyes even bluer, heavy shadow and thick mascara that made them pop, and a C-cup push-up bra providing cleavage and a bold display of her assets, something she'd never have dared show anyone, under a barely decent slimming silky tank and indecently short skirt with four-inch spike heels.

Yes, it was perfect, exactly the kind of woman that would have Cameron drooling, chasing her down, and spilling all his secrets. She heard the toilet flush and took in the stall door that opened. The woman had short dark hair, a mass of curls, a short knit skirt that appeared painted on, spike heels, and a skintight tank showing her generous bust. Yes, she definitely fit in.

"I swear these shoes are going to be the end of me, but the guys love 'em. Gets me those big tips, so I guess in the end it's worth it, although not sure my feet think the same." She had a deep, husky voice and was wiping a dark smudge under her eye from her thick mascara. Then she turned, giving Naomi a view of her curvy body and the way the skirt eased over her rounded butt and mile-long legs. The woman didn't just have a great figure; she had muscle and was perfectly toned. She winked at Naomi. "You one of the new girls?"

It took her a minute as she started to sweat. "Hoping to be. I'm here to meet with Pete. Although I don't have a lot of experience waiting tables, I really need the work," she said, cringing, realizing she may have gone a little overboard. She hoped it didn't sound too desperate.

The woman rolled her eyes and crossed her arms. "You should fit right in. Not to worry. It's about the looks, honey. Everything else can be taught." She gestured to Naomi's getup. "Yup, one look at you and the interview will be over." She leaned in the mirror again, dragging a deep red painted nail under her eye as if there was something there. "Just flash him a smile, and if you need to, tell him you've waited tables before over in Rock Springs. Can't see it getting that far, though. Pete's about the looks and whether you've got the heat and can sell it. Just let him get an eyeful of that cleavage and you'll be a shoe in."

She tapped the counter. "Just a word of advice, hon: If you really want to work here, the pay isn't great. If that's what you're counting on, go get a job at Smitty's family restaurant down the road. Here it's about the tips, which are exceptional, but it comes at a cost. The men providing said tips are pigs coming in off the rigs and are as free with their hands as they are with their wallets. As long as you understand that, you'll do just fine. Taffy is my name," she said, leaning against the counter. Of course she was waiting for something from Naomi.

"Julie," she spat out, feeling her heart kick up from the lie that had begun. She should have put more thought into it. Julie what? Her hands were sweaty. Her adrenaline surged.

"Nice to meet you, Julie. Hope you get the job," Taffy said before leaving.

Naomi took one last look in the mirror, lifted the strap of her small clutch over her shoulder, and said, "Show time."

She'd practiced walking in these spike heels for days, but she teetered a second as she took a step. Maybe getting the job wouldn't be the challenge; it would be staying upright in these ridiculously high shoes.

THE MUSIC WAS PULSING EVEN through the closed door of the back office. The room was ordinary, with an old scratched-up desk, a small steel safe in the corner, and an old four-drawer file cabinet. Turned out the man was named Dean, not Pete. The only thing she'd figured out was that he used to play sports, either a former boxer or hockey player, she couldn't remember which he'd said when she'd first stumbled in, reeling at the change in script. She'd done her homework on Pete and was thrown. Thinking on her feet wasn't really her strong suit. That was her sister Scarlett, who was a pain in the ass but had a skill Naomi coveted.

"So you've worked for Mr. Donnelly for how long?" Naomi said.

Dean didn't look up from where he rested his forearms on the desk, a pen in hand, writing something in a note-book. It was odd. He set the pen down and leaned back in the heavily padded older chair. It squeaked. His face was free of emotion and hard. Yikes!

"Why is it that I'm starting to feel as if I'm the one being interviewed?" He was studying her, and she didn't have a clue whether he was amused or ready to tell her to get lost.

She swallowed. Things were fast spiraling to the edge of a precipice where one of two things would happen: The opportunity she'd only just stepped into would be gone or, by some miracle, she'd get a pass. Unfortunately, she realized it would likely be the former, and that had her mind reeling, grasping at anything instead of remaining calm so she could nail this interview.

"Sorry, just curious. Always have been," she said. "Guess it's one of my faults. I tend to ask questions when nervous." She was sitting ramrod straight, her chest out, and sweat was dripping from her underarms. She leaned forward, going right to plan C, giving him an eyeful. He didn't seem interested at all. It was as if he was completely unaffected by her. He had to be a monk, or maybe it was the fact that Naomi didn't have a clue how to entice a guy. None of this was the reaction she'd expected. She was completely out of her element. She was drowning and sinking fast.

He lifted his pen again, and she could see the neat penmanship from where she sat. Odd for a guy to be focused on so much detail. "So you've waited tables in Rock Creek, where?" Direct and to the point.

She felt her throat close up and tried to think of all the places in Rock Creek, a place she'd been to only a handful of times. She couldn't remember the name of one damn place. "Bottoms Up," she finally said, recalling the roadside sign of a half-naked country gal with cutoffs that showed off more of her rounded ass than they covered. She was proud of herself and smiled brightly as she wrapped her hands over her crossed legs, just barely stopping herself from batting her lashes.

The man looked up. He had blue eyes and hair so short

it was almost buzzed. This time he smiled. His eyes danced, and her stomach knotted, because something wasn't right. "Yeah?" He actually laughed, controlled and rough, and she could feel her jaw tighten as he flicked the pen in his fingers and leaned back again, the smile now gone. "So when exactly was this?" He clicked the pen a couple more times, and her eyes went right there.

She was in a panic, in shock, and for a minute she thought she might puke from her nerves as she searched her mind for something, anything. "Two, three months ago." Her voice squeaked, completely rattled now. "I was at a small coffeehouse before that…"

His gaze was so deep. "Why is it that I think you're trying to blow smoke up my ass? I know everyone who works and has worked at Bottoms Up for the last five years, and, sweetheart, that ain't you." He wasn't smiling now, and his eyes had a look that said she was fucking with the wrong guy. "Coming in here and wasting my time by lying through your teeth to get a job, I ain't got time for that kind of bullshit." He gestured with his pen to a sign hammered to the wall, a drawing of a stickman in a hangman's noose. Below was written in red, *What happens to liars!*

It was something she'd never seen before, and her face flamed as she glanced back to him, wide eyed, seeing him organized and stacking papers into a pile, knowing he was so done with her.

"Word of advice," he said. "If you're going to lie, at least do your fucking homework and don't pick a business owned by Mr. Donnelly." He then winked, set his pen down, and lifted both hands, putting his fingers together. It was a move she found intimidating. Oh, good Lord, she was so screwed. Now what?

"Okay, I'm sorry, I lied. The problem is that I've never waited a table before in my life, unless you count dinner at my parents', where I clear dirty dishes and put food on the table, which I've done countless times." She uncrossed her legs and slid to the edge of the chair, her hands on the edge of the desk as desperation now threatened to strangle her. "I just really need this job and know places won't hire unless you have experience, but how am I supposed to get experience if you won't give me a chance? Please." Her voice squeaked. She was considering getting down on her knees and begging, anything to get him to look at her or at least give her one more chance, feeling the door closing on any chance of getting close to Cameron Donnelly. The man was untouchable, and the opening was closing before her. She'd never get another shot.

No such luck. The man was made of steel as if he didn't have an ounce of compassion for anyone. In fact, he was shaking his head, his expression set, as he started to lean forward to stand up. Next she knew, she'd be dismissed and the door would slam shut in her face.

Then the door at her back opened, and Cameron Donnelly, six foot two, with lean muscle, impeccably groomed, and better looking in person, if that was possible, stepped in. It was one of those moments where everything happened at once. He took in the room with his shrewd gaze, wondering yet knowing at the same time. His shirt-sleeves were rolled up, and the top buttons of his crisp white dress shirt were undone. He oozed something that had Naomi struggling to take a breath. How was it possible a man could affect her this way? Then she realized as she beamed up at him that he hadn't given her a second glance.

"I need you over in Laramie tomorrow," he said. "Handle the partners meeting for me. Make sure no issues arise this time." He pulled keys from the desk drawer and lifted a suit jacket she hadn't seen hanging from a hook on the wall. It was black and tailored and fit him like a glove. He still hadn't looked her way, not a glance, nothing, not an acknowledgement that she existed. Odd, considering how hot she looked. That definitely didn't help her confidence.

"Just finishing here now so I can be on my way…" Dean said. He lifted his wrist, glancing at his watch. "I'd say fifteen, tops."

"The situation's been handled?" Cameron was pulling at his cuffs.

Both men were carrying on as if she didn't even exist. It was so cryptic, and she wished she'd thought to record this. Her cell phone was slipped in her handbag, and it would be so easy to feign a call and turn it on. Then both men were staring at her. Cameron cleared his throat, not a smile, nothing. It really had a way of making a girl feel she wasn't wanted.

Dean stood up. The man was tall, handsome in a hard sort of way but not even close to oozing the attraction that seemed to make up Cameron Donnelly. No wonder women flocked to him. Fell prey to him.

"Thank you for coming, Miss…." Dean didn't offer his hand, and she knew in that panicked second she was being dismissed.

"Parker, Julie Parker. Please, I know I shouldn't have said I had experience and that I worked at a place I haven't, but I swear if you give me a chance, you won't regret it. I'm a quick learner, and I'll work hard."

Cameron glanced once to Dean and said only "You got this?" Then he started to the door.

This was going from bad to worse, and she had about half a second, she figured, before her opportunity was gone forever. She didn't think, she reacted. She jumped from the chair, swaying on those ridiculous heels and reaching out. She touched his arm, feeling the expensive dark cloth of his suit jacket. His eyes went to her hand, and she felt him flinch from her touch—something else she hadn't expected. He didn't look at her until she pulled her hand away. His eyes were green, an odd shade, and there was nothing friendly there. He was hard, unforgiving, alpha, and she was so screwed.

"Please, Mr. Donnelly, give me a chance. I promise you will not regret this. A week. One week! One day! And then if I don't show you I can do a good job, you can let me go." She was usually more convincing, but he was giving her nothing.

He glanced over her head to Dean, and they exchanged a look.

"She lied," Dean said. "Was just about to explain the policy." He gestured again to the homemade sign.

Cameron was looking straight through her as if she didn't exist. "I don't like liars and don't want the kind of trouble that always comes with a liar." He gestured to the open door and started to step away.

This was now at the stage where she was so fucking screwed that pride and dignity didn't have a place anymore. "I get it, and I never planned to come in and lie and say I had experience, but I was also expecting to be interviewed by Pete, who would have been more interested in how I looked and how much skin I showed. My experience wouldn't have been something that mattered… I'm not a liar, I don't lie, but I really need this job." She was rambling, and her face was burning under all the caked-on makeup that made her eyes itch. She wondered for a moment whether they could see through some of her half-truths, her lies, and all the bullshit she was tossing out to turn the tables so this would go her way.

Cameron still hadn't moved. He was watching her, and

she didn't have a fucking clue what the hell he was think-ing. That had the sweat beading between her shoulder blades.

"One day then, please," she said. "I beg you, give me a chance. I swear I'm a hard worker. You won't regret it."

The silence continued. It was only her panicked breath she could hear. She watched as Cameron wiped his face, and all that she could think was that he appeared tired. She didn't have a clue whether she'd gotten through to him. Maybe he'd have her thrown out now with a warning never to come back.

"Don't do it," she heard Dean say from behind her just as Cameron stepped out the door.

He then turned back to them, his hand in the air, his eyes closed a second before looking over to Dean. "Give her the job, but if she pulls anything, get rid of her." Then he was gone without looking her way or giving her anything to say, "Okay, I see you."

Lies, deception, greed. Yes, she wasn't being honest, but then, he was all of that and more. He deserved to be exposed, and Naomi Parker had no doubt now that she'd be able to scrape together the story that would officially take Cameron Donnelly down.

Chapter Two

The amber bourbon stared at him from the square-cut glass. He dropped in some ice and lifted it. "You sure about what you found?" he said, resting his hand on the large center island in his spacious kitchen, which opened into a huge living room with a two-story rock fireplace. The great room was open above.

"One hundred percent positive," Dean said from over the phone. "There's no doubt Pete was using the bar as a one-stop shop for knockoff fentanyl and street-grade oxy, among other things."

Dean was his brother, a former boxer turned DEA agent who'd burnt out and hit rock bottom after too many years undercover and too many years shooting up. He was now sober after two stints in rehab, and he was the only person Cameron completely trusted. The man was two years older, a five-time graduate of the school of hard knocks, but he'd always had Cameron's back, sober or drunk. Family first, scumbags second.

"Not sure how much or how long he's been running it

through your place," Dean said, "but it was enough that he'd established a nice sideline, a lot of cash changing hands. Could still be problems. Expect a few of those roughnecks at the bar are regular users, and there's your staff, the waitresses, bartender, bouncer, dancers… Shall I go on?"

The phone was in the center of the counter on speaker, and Cameron listened to Dean, furious at himself for missing the fact that a man who'd worked for him for years, who had made himself seem indispensable, had abused his trust and lied to his face. He hated liars, and it angered him more that he still hadn't learned his lesson. Trusting a liar had nearly cost him everything—all because of a woman.

"Any trouble getting rid of him?" He took a swallow, welcoming the bite, the burn.

"No, no trouble. But you're sure you don't want me to make a call to the Feds, lock him up? It's your call, but he's just going to be selling somewhere else, running his racket. Best to end Pete's career once and for all. The chances of some blowback on you are almost certain."

He was shaking his head. How could he explain to anyone that he was done with the spotlight, with exposing himself and his life? Never again would he have anyone looking anywhere into his personal and business life, scrutinizing every aspect of what he did and didn't do. It was an intrusion, a destruction he'd never allow in his life again. No, anonymity was better. He'd walk away from everything else.

"Do whatever you want now that he isn't working for me," Cameron said. "Bust him somewhere away from my businesses, where there will be no questions or spotlight shone anywhere in my direction." He rested his hand over the button to disconnect. "Just make sure all the locks get changed tonight at every one of my businesses, and you find out if anyone else is trying to run something out of my places. But I mean it: Get everything away from me and my businesses. I want peace, and I sure as shit cannot go through another scandal. I run a clean place, all of them. I pay my taxes. I, unlike every other business out there, play by the rules, and I want it to stay that way."

"I get that, Cam, I really do, but you need to let it go. It was over a year ago. Move on. This isn't the same thing. You didn't do anything wrong here, and people will see that and know—"

"You're full of shit. People don't give a shit about the truth. The only thing they see is my name, my business, and it doesn't matter that I knew nothing of it. It's the perception, and that alone is all anyone needs to create a twisted version of reality. Some will say, 'Hey, he must have done something wrong, because he's been in trouble before,' and people feed off that."

Those people Cameron had thought were his friends had become part of the problem and turned on him, because even though people said otherwise, everyone still judged for perceived deeds instead of the unmistakable content of his character. They lived for the gossip, the drama, even if it wasn't anywhere close to the truth. Except Dean, who'd always walked his own road, made up his own mind.

"Okay, I hear you. I get the fact that the wound has festered and you're not ready to say 'Fuck you all' to the world and let it go, so I'll coddle you on this. Maybe I'll start sugarcoating everything for you until you rediscover those tender sensibilities that make you so damn pretty."

"Oh, fuck you." He wanted to smack his brother

through the phone as he swirled the glass of bourbon and then set it on the counter. At the same time, he was feeling better at the way his brother didn't coddle him but made fun of how prickly he'd become.

"Yeah, you too," Dean said. "By the way, I hired that chick."

He was blank, staring at the phone, wondering what the hell his brother was talking about. "Sorry…" He was shaking his head even though his brother couldn't see as he leaned on the counter, his hand wrapped around the glass again.

"The looker in the office, you know, the one I warned you not to hire. But hey, I saw the look on your face, buying into her sob story. Jesus Murphy, man, when will you learn a pretty face is akin to the final stake being driven right into your nuts? Girls will be the end of you."

Crude, too, his brother. Too many years living and breathing with the scum of the earth. He still didn't know who he was talking about as he scrambled to think of where he'd been today, yesterday… Oh, yeah, it hit him, the pathetic thing who'd begged and pleaded while his gut had been screaming trouble. "Well, keep an eye on her. If she does anything, bounce her."

This time, he hit the disconnect button before his brother could call him an idiot again. Maybe Dean was right. Maybe he should listen and bounce the girl before she started her shift, before he fell neck deep in something that wouldn't just leave him burned and scarred but would take a piece of him he'd never get back.

He took in his sprawling rancher on forty acres ten miles outside of Casper. All four thousand square feet were done in browns and oranges, comfortable and rustic, a place he'd owned for five years, though he'd nearly lost all of it because of Lori. What was it about women that they all seemed to be playing him or hunting him? Didn't matter who they were. As far as he was concerned, they were always working an angle, always wanting something.

Chapter Three

"I got the job!" Naomi was still giddy, and she tapped her steering wheel again, fighting the urge to bounce up and down as she drove, thinking over the unbelievable turn of events. She'd managed to pull off a miracle of epic proportions, landing an undercover job without having any experience or even the first clue as to what she was walking into. Silence seemed to stretch on the other end of the phone. "Are you still there?" She was staring at the Bluetooth of her dash to see whether she'd lost her cell connection.

There was a cough in the background, and then a door closed. "Yeah, I'm still here. Honestly, Naomi, I never thought you could pull it off." The shock was still there in her editor's voice. She'd stopped herself from sharing any part of how she'd blown the interview. Best keep that to herself, considering she was still getting nothing.

"Flory, you're making me feel a little underappreciated," she said, her joy dimming.

"Sorry, Naomi, it's just… Wow, seriously, big wow." She laughed deeply then.

Naomi could picture her editor, Flory Hunter, a divorced woman in her forties with two grown kids and one teenager, short and plump, with deep red hair, an open bag of Doritos likely on her desk. It was rare to see her without one. She swore that was all the woman ate, and she didn't share.

"I'm sorry," Flory said again. "Congratulations. Good for you. I seriously never expected you could pull this off, but I have to tell you that was the easy part, because getting close to Cameron will not be easy. No, it will be almost impossible." Flory was the head of a team of reporters, and she was who Naomi had been interning under. The Cameron Donnelly story that had died out the previous year was something Naomi had pushed for. Everyone else wasn't interested.

"Well, Cameron was the one to give me the job, in fact, so I've already met him and now have access," she said. Did her nose grow? She ground her teeth over that twist of facts, considering she didn't have a clue when she'd see him, if she'd see him, or how she'd get close to him, let alone get him to see her, talk to her, and even smile her way. He seemed to be made of something impenetrable.

There was tapping in the background, and she stared at the gray of the highway. She wasn't far from home. She was exhausted and needed to wash off the makeup, free her breasts from the restrictive push-up bra that had turned them into every man's wet dream, and figure out what to tell her family about her sudden change in hair color.

"Okay, just hang tight for a second," Flory said. Naomi could hear typing in the background, and she wondered what her editor was doing. "Just waiting for an okay," she said. Her voice faded off as if she was typing and thinking, and Naomi then wondered whether she'd heard her right.

"You mean this story hasn't been okayed?" Her hands squeezed the steering wheel of her little ten-year-old Subaru.

Silence again. What was that sound she'd heard?

"Well, yes and no. Honestly, Naomi, when you pitched the idea of digging into the life of Cameron and uncovering the truth, the lies, the money, the fraud, everything written in the local papers last year before the scandal died a slow death, I thought you were crazy. I never thought you could have the kind of womanly experience needed to pull something like this off. Impressed is beyond what I feel right now—and okay, here we go. Just got the preemptive okay from the CEO, but with a provisional that he could pull the plug at any time if you don't find anything meaningful. He also has a word of caution: Do this right. I'm going to add my own words of wisdom for you, too, Naomi. Be careful, and tell your family, your parents, what you're up to, considering you're putting yourself in a situation I would doubt they'd be comfortable with. I'd put my foot down if it were my daughter."

She heard the warning, and at the same time she knew exactly what her parents would say. No!

"I'll think about it, but it's best if they don't know. Besides, I'll have the story done and wrapped up before they even have a chance to worry, so no sense upsetting anyone here."

"Mm-hmm" was all she heard. A chair squeaked. "Listen, when do you start? I'd like to go over a few things with you about where to focus."

"Well, I have the story outlined already. I'll find out everything I can about how Cameron Donnelly is one of the pioneers in discovering loopholes in Wyoming, making it into the Cayman of the prairies. Wyoming has grandiose loopholes guaranteeing anonymity, creditor protection, and no state tax, making the wealthy wealthier and the poor poorer, bringing an end to the middle class. I'll find everything. There's a file cabinet in the back of the bar. I'll start there and work my way to getting closer to Donnelly. Then I'll figure out how to find evidence that ties him to all those Hong Kong import/export companies, the Chinese money, the oil tycoons, the scammers, and the money he's skimming off the top. I'll find it, and this story will expose him to the world for the enemy of the people that he is."

She didn't have a clue how she'd start to unravel why Donnelly, who owned a stable of businesses, a bar, a dry cleaner, a convenience store, a coffee house in Rock Creek, and, as she'd learned tonight, a titty bar and who knows what else, would be at the forefront of funneling and hiding foreign money in a state with the loosest laws in the country. It was a story that could and would launch her career, earning her a nomination if not an award for something that would rock the nation. She was excited and at the same time scared as hell for what she was getting herself into. There was silence again until she heard crunching. Yup, she was eating Doritos.

"Maybe we should have talked about this a bit. Honey, that isn't the story, and you're not Jane Mayer, Barbara Ehrenreich, or even Barbara Walters. This is a small-town paper that doesn't have the kind of resources to vet a story like that."

What? "Well, of course that's the story—and vetting… That's why I'm working this undercover, to get all the evidence. I'll find the paper trail, wear a wire—"

"Stop right now, Naomi. You're going off onto something that very few investigative reporters would take on, let alone have the skill to do. This is a small town, remember, and this piece is about his human side, the personal, the dirt. Find out, okay? So, game plan. You check in every day and report to me everything you find out. And, Naomi, do I need to remind you to be careful?"

Her boss was older, motherly, and a woman who'd at one time chased some of the biggest political scandals in history. She'd seen some of her stuff and knew she'd taken a lot of heat. She now worked at a small-time paper, which was a step down from the *Washington Post*, which had made her career. Another story, she was sure, and one she knew Flory would never share.

"I will, and don't worry," Naomi said. She'd do the story and still dig up the evidence to show it was so much more than just personal dirt. She'd prove what an asshole Cameron Donnelly was.

"Easier said than done, Naomi. Hope you realize you now are out of the kiddie pool and are in fact swimming with the sharks. So be sharp, stay smart, and call anytime if you get into trouble. And tell your parents." Then she hung up.

Naomi could see cars and pickups outside as she drove past the main house to her cabin, one of three her father had built for her and her two older sisters, Taz and Ivy, to keep them close. Taz was now married, though, and living in Denver.

That was when she realized what she'd forgotten. *Oh, shit!* She'd just missed Sunday dinner, a tradition in her family that could be skipped only because of work or illness. She noted that the screen door was open, but she didn't spare a glance to see who stepped out, her mom, her dad, or maybe one of her sisters.

All she knew was that she was barely decent except for the coat pulled over her skimpy outfit, the sneakers on her feet, and the heavy-handed makeover that was sure to have her pounded with questions. Her stilettos were in the bag on the passenger seat, which was a good thing, as those would also have brought a flood of questions. She stepped out of the car, holding her coat closed, lifting the bag over her shoulder as she hurried.

She could hear someone coming, and she decided it was best to not look back as she jumped up on the porch, her hand on the doorknob.

"Naomi, seriously, is that you?"

She darted a glance back to see her sister Taz was back from her honeymoon. Her husband, Jerry, was behind her. They were tanned and relaxed, walking hand in hand, so close, so in love. When they saw her face, shock was evident in both their expressions.

"Hey there, you two. Sorry, forgot about dinner. When did you get back?" She stepped inside her cottage and wanted to close the door. At the same time, she took in her sister and the odd look on her face. Jerry, mister tall, dark, and extremely good looking, appeared amused.

"We flew in yesterday, drove down this morning. Missed you all and wanted to catch up—and good God, girl, what did you do to yourself?" Taz stepped in the open door of her cottage. Naomi had rested her bag on the kitchen table and was about to slip out of her coat, but she thought better of it. They were staring at her again as if they were at a loss for words. She didn't like the focus on her, instead wishing it could be the other way around.

"You like it?" She pressed her hand to the back of her dyed hair and smiled. Her eyes were burning from the contact lenses she wasn't used to wearing, or maybe it was the heavy shadow, liner, and thick mascara.

Jerry had a pained expression on his face, and Taz was no longer smiling as she allowed her gaze to drop down to Naomi's toes, taking in all of her. "Not sure what this is, this new you, but…are you in some kind of trouble?"

"What? No!" She was taken aback and worried now

about the impression they had. "Just a story I'm working on, and…" She needed to shut up, because even Jerry seemed beyond curious, as if he was about to lay into her, question her, and demand some answers.

"Story? What kind of story has you dying your hair and painting yourself up like…" Taz was gesturing at her, and Naomi was glad she'd had the forethought to keep her coat closed as Taz eyed her up and down. Then she noticed Jerry looking at her bag and obviously spotting her heels. He motioned to Taz, and she lifted one out, her face in complete shock as she took them in. They were black with red soles. A work of art, really, but pure torture on her feet.

"I think you'd better tell us what kind of story has you changing your appearance and wearing shoes no sane person could walk in. And what are you wearing under that coat?" Taz had crossed her arms.

Jerry, who had yet to say two words, finally piped up with embarrassment. "Naomi, what kind of story are you working on that has you appearing like…?"

Her face burned when she realized his implication. She didn't know him well and couldn't help feeling put on the spot. "Seriously, you two? Listen, why don't I get changed, wash this off, and come on over…"

She stopped talking as her sister's expression became one of disbelief. "Naomi, I swear right now that you need to tell us what this is, and what are you wearing? What are you hiding under that—" Taz stepped toward her and rested her hand over hers, lifting her coat and seeing the skintight, indecently short skirt.

No choice now. Naomi allowed the coat to fall open. Even Jerry appeared shocked.

"What kind of story has you dressing like a hooker?" Taz said. "Please tell me you're not…"

"No! Good grief, Taz. I'm not pretending to be a hooker." No, she was working at a seedy bar, dressed like one of the strippers, serving men who were freer with their hands than they were on the streets with a prostitute.

Jerry stepped forward, taking her in. He appeared uneasy as he wiped his chin. She could see he was thinking some things she probably wasn't going to like. "Not a hooker, but something not far from it. What kind of undercover story is this?" he said, his hand on Taz, who still appeared as if she were reeling from shock.

"It's a story, a good story, and that's all you need to know." This was her career, and she wasn't going to answer to her family or anyone about what she was doing.

"Stop, Naomi!" Taz said sharply, her hand up. "I think you need to tell us what exactly you've gotten yourself into. Since when do you go undercover for a story? I thought you were interning, just helping out with a column or something…" She trailed off, and Naomi wondered how much her family even knew about what she did. By the confused look on Taz's face, she wondered if they'd even read anything she'd written. The thought of it actually bothered her, their lack of interest.

"Columns are not something I've ever done. Yes, I'm interning, but it's always local pieces, fluff stuff, community news and goings-on. But not this time, and I have the support of my paper. This story is big, and no one can know anything about it. That's why it's undercover, investigative journalism." She knew from the exchange between Taz and Jerry that they weren't about to just walk away without some answers from her, so she lifted her hands, then realized her breasts were indecently exposed, so she crossed her arms over them. "It's an undercover assignment. I'm not a hooker but a waitress, is all."

She slipped off her coat and rested it over the chair,

feeling for a moment as if she were standing naked. She may as well have been, considering her outfit left little to the imagination, but then, that had been the entire purpose. Let her body do the talking. When she had Cameron's undying attention, he'd be putty in her hands. After all, what guy couldn't resist a gorgeous woman? She flashed a smile, but neither Taz nor her husband warmed. They were both staring at her as if she'd lost her mind.

"Whatever it is you're doing, Naomi, it doesn't take a genius to figure out that the way you're dressed, you're putting yourself in a bad position. I wonder if you've really considered the consequences. Dressed that way, waitressing, you'd need to be working in a bar, strip club, or…" Jerry said, and she could see him thinking, digging deep to figure out what she was up to as he stood with Taz, his hands around her now. Taz was still holding one of the stilettos, resting it on the table. "From what I know of you girls, your parents would not be okay with this, and I wonder if maybe you really understand what you're getting yourself into." He was shaking his head and staring at her as if she were a child.

Now this was pissing her off. "You make me sound as if I haven't got any sense at all. Of course I understand, and you're blowing this all out of proportion. It's just a job, undercover. I'll get the story, be done and finished, and no one needs to worry about anything."

Jerry didn't seem convinced, though, and Taz was giving all her attention to him. Then she slowly turned her head to Naomi. "You either tell us where it is you're working and what story this is, or I'm telling Mom and Dad," Taz said. From Jerry's expression, he seemed very much on board with his wife.

"Taz, you wouldn't do that to me."

Jerry still had his hand around Taz's waist as he

stepped forward. "Just a second, both of you. Naomi, your sister's right, and I'm also pretty sure you have no idea what it is you're walking into. I doubt very much, dressed as you are, that you'd be able to protect yourself if something happened—guys pawing at you, or worse." He was shaking his head, taking in Taz and then Naomi. "You and all your sisters have been sheltered. I just never realized how much. I doubt very much you have any idea what to do if something goes sideways, which, dressed as you are, is way up on the list of quite likely."

This was ridiculous. She was a grown woman, twenty-four, and she knew and had seen some pretty shocking things. She'd been right to think she needed to keep this to herself. "Fine, it's a place in Casper," she said. They said nothing, waiting for her to give them everything. "A place called The Wilde Horse. It's a—"

"Strip club owned by Cameron Donnelly," Jerry said, then swore. "It's where all the oil grunts hang out, blow off steam, and look for sex."

Taz stared at her as if she'd lost her mind.

Chapter Four

She was three hours into an eight-hour shift that had
started at ten in the morning. Naomi couldn't
believe how jammed the place was for that time of
day. Who could have known a bar would open that early
and girls would be taking off their clothes for guys sitting in
chairs, ogling them? It seemed as if half the patrons were
oil workers with cash to throw away, hands that had no
boundaries, and mouths that were downright shocking. It
wasn't as if Naomi hadn't heard her share of rough
language, bad words, and in fact she could spit out a few of
her own, but it was as if these guys had forgotten everything their mothers had taught them, with hands that had
touched and pinched her ass, slid up her thigh when she'd
delivered a tray of drinks, and boldly tossed a few hundred
her way after some horny guy had asked her to hike up her
skirt and take a seat on his lap, then slip out back to the
narrow, dirty alleyway, where garbage was piled sky high.

The men startled her, and she hated to admit that it
shook her up to be degraded in such a way. She'd ended up
walking away to where she now stood at the bar, her feet

aching, questioning her sanity. What the hell was she thinking? Maybe there was a better way. What kind of man owned a place like this?

"How's it going there, hon? Julie, right?" It was Taffy, the dark-haired hottie with the short mop, wearing a black tank, a short tight skirt, and red stilettos. Her gold hoops were big and touched her shoulders.

"My feet are killing me, and I'm sure I'm black and blue from all the guys who've pinched my ass. Oh, and sticky from the tray of drinks I spilled the first order because I wasn't prepared for the fact that the asshole by the stage, all sweaty and in bad need of a haircut and shave, felt he had the right to stick his hand up my skirt, over my ass." She took in the frown on the bartender's face. Joe was dark haired, about five ten, from the Cree reservation, she thought. He was listening now, though he'd said nothing when she'd come back with the spilled tray of drinks, looking for more.

"You get used to it, sort of," Taffy said. "Hey, Joe, where's Pete? He's supposed to be out here watching so these guys don't get out of hand. There's no touching, remember?" she snapped, and Joe rolled his eyes.

"Oh, you mean the written rule or the unwritten one where you ask me to turn away and ignore the touching because of the extra tips?" He sounded like a smart ass, and Taffy leveled him with a dark look.

"New girl, remember?" That was all she said. Whatever the exchange between them, Naomi was hard pressed to figure out what it meant. She was stuck on Pete, the guy she'd been supposed to meet, the man she'd not yet laid eyes on.

Joe shrugged. "Was fired, is all I heard, all I was told. Hasn't been replaced." He gestured with his chin to the men who filled the darkened bar. "I've been keeping an eye out."

Naomi took in the bartender, and for the first time she wanted to tell him to fuck himself. Maybe Taffy figured it out, as she smiled at her, leaning on the counter.

"Maybe you could do more than watch and actually get your ass out there," she said. "You know the rules of the bar, no touching, and she's new."

Joe only grunted and then rested a pitcher of draft on Naomi's tray along with two shots of tequila and glasses. Then he pointed. "Table in the corner over there has been waiting. Take it on over."

Taffy rested her hand on the tray when Naomi went to lift it. "Leave it. I'll take it. Joe, don't be an asshole. Go and deal with those roughnecks. You've only managed to prove you can be a prick, so give Julie a break, would you?"

Instead of Taffy taking the tray, Joe did. He walked across the darkened bar, illuminated by the lights from the stage, just as she heard the announcement that Heather from Houston was coming on. As the curtain opened, two things went through Naomi's mind: Today was the first time she'd seen a stripper, and she was starting to rethink the wisdom of working in this bar.

"Don't you worry none," Taffy said. "Joe's done that to all of us. Kind of his way, I think, of tough loving the girls. First day on the job, so he's seeing if you have what it takes to cut it or if you need to go running out the door. It's his test. You must have passed, as you're still here. He wouldn't have let nothing happen."

Naomi noticed Joe saying something to the table of rowdies and the guy who'd propositioned her with words she'd never heard before. She could feel her face burning again as she thought of it. Then he started back toward the bar. He was big, stocky, and had arms that could toss any man out.

"Yeah, well, excuse me if I don't believe you," Naomi said. "You know that one of them actually tossed me a hundred and expected me to hop out back with him?" She was still mad—no, furious, for the first time feeling how degraded a woman could feel. It wasn't a great feeling, and it had her thinking what it would take for a woman to take that money and let a total stranger use her body. She swallowed the bile when a hand touched her arm.

"Oh, they try, but if it happens again, you tell Joe," Taffy said. "I wonder what happened to Pete."

Naomi wanted to say she didn't know and tell her about the other man, Dean, when someone slid up beside her.

"Vodka straight," the man said, "and is Pete around?" He was tall, with dark hair, clean cut, in blue jeans and a dress shirt. He had a nice smile.

"Sure there, honey." Taffy slipped around the bar and pulled out a glass, then poured a splash of vodka and set it on the counter. "Just heard Pete no longer works here. Can I help you with something?" She was smiling brightly, leaning across the bar now as Joe reappeared, but Taffy gave him no mind, her hand on her waist, chewing gum, staring at the man in a way that seemed overly interested and flirty.

"Know where he went?" The man downed the vodka, pulled out his wallet, and tossed down a twenty.

"No, but you may want to ask Joe. He seems to have all the answers." Taffy looked back over her shoulder as Joe rested Naomi's tray on the counter. He looked from her to Taffy and finally to the man, and that was when she spotted Cameron coming in the back door, wearing a leather jacket. He pulled off his shades and took everyone and everything in—everyone except her, that is, as if she'd suddenly become invisible to a man like him, as if she were someone he didn't even recognize.

She didn't hear what Joe or Taffy said as she watched Cameron walk away and through the door to the hallway that led to the back office.

"Julie, didn't you hear me?"

"Sorry?" she said as Taffy stared at her and then over to the door Cameron had just walked through.

Taffy shook her head. "Yeah, that's the boss. And a word of advice: That's one man you definitely don't want to cross."

Chapter Five

There was so much crap, files and papers and ledgers along with two USB sticks he'd found in the old desk drawer. How could he have ignored what had been happening right under his nose? Hindsight was a funny thing.

So was handling everything himself.

There was a knock on the door. Must've been Dean. "It's about time you got your ass down here," Cameron said. "Was hoping you'd…"

"Sorry, Mr. Donnelly. It's just me."

He turned to the female voice, the blonde. Her hair was hiked high in a ponytail, though it still hung past her butt. She was a looker with an amazing body that skimpy outfit did little to hide, with curves and everything guys in a place like this would give their last dollar just to have a minute, an hour, or any time with.

She stepped inside, and he was trying to figure out what her name was.

"Yes, what can I do for you…?" He left it hanging, because he didn't really care who she was or what her name was. He had more important things to focus on, like fixing a problem that wasn't even his.

"Julie," she said and then strode to the desk, hand on her hip, flaunting all her assets. It was something she should have saved for the guys in the bar. He wasn't interested. She was just another pretty face and a whole lot of trouble.

He turned away. "Julie, are you lost?" he said, slamming the file cabinet closed and dumping the files, papers, books, everything into a box he'd rested on the piece of shit desk from a century ago that had come with this place, a place he still couldn't believe he inadvertently owned. He didn't look up to hear her heels on the dirty concrete floor and notice that she was no longer posing for him. The tension and energy in the room had changed.

"No. Sorry, Mr. Donnelly. Just wanted to thank you again for hiring me and giving me a chance. I really need the work and again am sorry for what happened," she said.

He just stared at her then, trying to piece it together. "Uh-huh, well, okay." What was it about her that seemed off? "Is that all?" He stopped what he was doing, looking over to her, wondering why she was still there.

The heavy coating of shadow and thick mascara seemed pasted on, adding to everything that didn't seem to fit. Not that he hadn't noticed the legs, the ass, but that was it. The sex kitten look was far from meaningful. Maybe at one time it had done something for him. Not anymore.

"I, uh…" She seemed lost for words as he turned his back, opening the second drawer. She was still there when he glanced back. She was beginning to seem like a pain in the ass.

"Julie, is it? I'm at a loss. Is there something you need, something else that maybe isn't working here for you?"

Another woman trying to find her way closer to him, he figured. Where was Dean when he needed him?

"Mr. Donnelly, when I said to your associate that I had a lot of experience and told him I waited tables at Bottoms Up, I had no idea you owned it. I'm sorry. I just wanted to apologize again for lying. I listened to bad advice, believing I wouldn't even have a shot at a job if I told the truth that I had no experience. I believed the person who…"

"Who told you to lie?" He cut her off, as he was tired of this bullshit, and it was starting to sound like an excuse for bad behavior. He hated that shit. Deception was about the worst quality that existed, as far as he was concerned.

"It doesn't matter. It was just advice from someone who was trying to help me because of who I was interviewing with, Pete. That wasn't who I met, and I have to admit I was thrown. I believed that if asked about past work, I wouldn't get a chance otherwise." Her eyes were big, and she was blinking now, a lot.

"One of my employees?" he asked. Now he was certain he had someone else on his payroll pulling shit.

"I'm sorry, I won't tell you that. It wasn't something that was said to cause trouble. It was to help me—and that's not why I came back here."

He slammed the drawer closed. He was starting to get the feeling there was something else at play here, and he was being reeled into something he wasn't going to like. "Why did you come into this office? You saw me walk in, so you followed me? You're obviously working a shift, and I don't handle the day-to-day operations of who's on call, so get to it and then get your ass back out there or you can find yourself another job." He didn't care at this point whether he sounded like an asshole.

Her face colored. "I wanted to thank you for giving me a chance and tell you that you won't regret hiring me. I'll do a good job," she said, her hands linked together in front of her now, awkward.

He rested his arm on the top of the cheap metal cabinet. "The problem is, I'm already regretting it. If you want the truth, I wouldn't have hired you if I'd known you had no experience in a place like this." He looked up as he heard footsteps, and Dean walked in, slowing taking in the blonde standing in front of him.

"What's going on here?" Dean took only a second to take in every inch of the waitress before looking over to him.

"I need to get back to work. Thanks again, Mr. Donnelly," she said, stepping around Dean. The exchange was awkward as she slipped out of the office, her heels clattering down the hall.

His brother stepped in, gesturing with his thumb to the girl. "What was that about?" he asked.

Cameron just shook his head. "Not a clue, but something, I'm sure. Keep an eye on her, because something about that one screams trouble. It was something she said, too, about someone telling her to make up the story of working in a sleazy bar, as if you need that kind of experience on a resume." He rested his hand on the box of papers. "This is the last of it. I'm going to get this over to the accountant, let him go through it." He lifted the box as Dean slipped off his leather jacket and hung it on the hook behind the desk.

"The girl, you should have listened to me when I said don't do it. It's not too late, you know. Just say the word and she's out of here. Could bounce her now and save us all a huge headache." Dean could be a hard ass, but he also cut through all the bullshit and couldn't be bought, swayed, or persuaded by anyone.

"Maybe, just keep an eye out. Any problems, get rid of her." He started to the door, carrying the box.

"Hey, Cam, you really take a look at her? I'm telling you something is off about that chick that I can't put my finger on, exactly, but I've got this thing I can't shake in my head. It's this thing Dad said again and again: Sometimes what you see before you isn't how it really is. And my gut is screaming really loudly about that new waitress. No matter how she looks, there's something there, and no way a girl like that belongs in a place like this."

Chapter Six

"Shit, shit, shit." She was totally blowing this. She hurried down the darkened hallway, moving past a rig worker who gave her everything in his look, his hand touching her ass as she scooted past.

"Hey!" she said, then forced herself to paste a smile to her face when instead she wanted to puke from a touch that was far from wanted.

"Ah, come on, baby. Slow on down, there. Just want to have a conversation with you, is all." The man had thick dark hair and broad shoulders, and he appeared to be coming off a bender, with a two-day beard and rough gaze. He reeked from whatever booze he'd been downing, and she tried to place him from the group of jerks who had been pawing at her and making all kinds of lewd comments since she'd started.

"Look, I don't know you, and I don't want to have a conversation with you, so you just keep right on moving…"

He pressed in closer, pinning her to the wall, his face mere inches from hers, his arm resting above her head. She realized there was no one around, and for the first time she felt very real fear sneak up and start to choke her. She pressed her shaking hand to his chest as she tried to move him away, but he pressed closer, smiling, his breath reeking of cheap beer. She realized she was no match for him.

"I swear to God, if you don't back off, I will scream." Her voice was shaking, and then his hand pressed over her mouth as he pinned her arm above her head to the wall. His mouth lowered and moved to her ear.

"Now, darlin', I guarantee you you do not want to do that. Just be friendly to me and I'll make sure you're paid real well. We're just going to slip out the back and into the backseat of my car, and I'll show you what it is to be with a real man. I promise you'll even want more." His arm slipped around her like a steel band, holding her tight. She wanted to scream, but there was nothing but a muffled sound from behind his sweaty hand. Tears popped, and for a moment she went into a void of nothingness as he moved her. She saw the exit sign, and he would have her out that door and no one would know.

For the first time in her life, she couldn't move, she couldn't think. All her sound reasoning left, and she was stuck in the horror that something bad was happening. All she could see was that door coming closer, and there was nothing that would save her. Then it felt as if she'd been pushed or something. Her face hit the door jamb, her hand still pinned behind her, and then she was on the floor. There was a sound behind her. She wasn't sure what—fists, anger, shouting, something, and she just stared at her hand and the blood smeared there.

She couldn't feel anything except that she had to open her mouth to breathe. She saw two men in the shadows. Dean was pinning down the sweaty, stinking asshole who wasn't taking no for an answer. Her mind took in every-thing, and she just sat there, frozen, hearing a panicked breath and realizing it was hers. Then it was Cameron leaning down, squatting, concerned. She noticed his mouth moving, slow motion, and she couldn't make anything out. Then he had her in his arms, lifting her, and her legs were like jelly as he helped her down the corridor, walking through an open door to the back office. He sat her in a hardwood banker's chair wheeled over from against the corner.

He wasn't touching her now, and she started shaking.

"She okay?"

She heard a voice, Dean. She couldn't look up as she pressed her hand to her chest over her breasts, slouching, wishing she had a sweater or coat or something to put around herself. Maybe they knew, as Cameron shrugged out of his coat, leather, heavy, and slipped it around her. It was big and welcome and made her feel as if she could hide from everyone. She pulled at the front, covering her trembling now, but not from the cold.

"Julie."

She heard the name and didn't have a clue who they were talking to. She just stared at Cameron, who was careful not to touch her and said something to Dean. She kept her mouth open to breathe, feeling wet running from her nose. She wiped at it and saw fresh blood, a lot of it, on her hand. It was dripping now on the coat, the floor.

"Cops are called, on their way."

She looked up and saw Joe in the doorway and Taffy too, staring at her in horror. This was truly awful. A cloth was handed to her, and she just stared at it before Cameron lifted her hand to take the cloth and put both to her nose. That was when she felt the pain.

"Argh! Oh, my nose…"

Then a bag of ice appeared, another hand. Everyone was there.

"Hold this here. Call the paramedics." It was Cameron talking, and he pressed the pack of ice to the bridge of her nose.

She blinked, feeling her contact lenses pinching. She needed to get them out as she held the cloth to her nose, which was still bleeding and hurt like hell. Was her nose broken? It had to be, considering how much it hurt. She couldn't breathe out of it, but maybe that was more from the bleeding. From the pain that hit her, she thought there was something, and she was having trouble breathing, so she opened her mouth wider, gasping.

No, this couldn't be happening. "You know what?" she said. "I'm fine. No cops, no paramedics. I'll just clean myself up and…" What the hell was she doing? No one was talking. Everyone was staring at her as if she'd lost her mind.

"No one comes into a place of mine and hurts anyone who works for me," Cameron said. "If I hadn't come out of the office when I did, do you have any idea what was about to happen to you?"

She coughed and then yelped from the jarring pain, bringing a fire to her face.

"You were two steps from the door. He was dragging you out to rape you, maybe kill you and dump you. You have no fucking idea what the hell you got yourself into. I saw the fear, the panic, and I couldn't figure out why you weren't fighting him." He sounded like an asshole, like the unfeeling monster he'd been rumored to be.

"I froze," she blurted out, furious at herself now as she relived what happened. The moment the man had walked up, first looked at her, she should have…what? Then he touched her. She should have screamed then. The moment he pinned her to the wall, she should have fought, clawed, bit, punched, kicked, and she willed the image to her mind of everything she hadn't done. Why hadn't she kicked him, bit him, used her fists, her elbows? She should have screamed before his hand slipped over her mouth, and she was furious with herself. How could she have just let him drag her away? It was as if she'd frozen and forgotten everything she'd ever heard.

She couldn't explain to anyone why her muscles, her body, her mind hadn't cooperated, and the way Cameron was staring at her now, she wondered if he didn't in some way blame her.

"He was going to drag you out that door, and all you can say is you froze? That guy came in here looking for something. You're flaunting everything at him, and you have no fucking idea what kind of fire you're playing with. These guys are rough and work long hours, weeks at a stretch, and when they let loose, they forget every civilized thing they've ever been taught."

Cameron sounded like an asshole, and it really did sound as if he blamed her in some way. She didn't want to spend another minute here. She wanted to go home and shut the door and cry. She didn't want to talk to anyone, to explain and justify her reaction, her part in it.

"You think this is my fault," she said, and her throat ached, her chest burned. She prayed her family would never find out. Cameron was right; this didn't look good, and impressions were everything.

"He put his hands on you without your permission. This is not your fault," Taffy said as she stepped in, and man, did she look pissed. For a moment, Naomi was sure Taffy was going to hit Cameron or something. He backed away, and she realized it was Taffy holding the icepack to her face.

There was a tap at the door. She couldn't see who it was until the cop stepped into the small, now crowded office. He was older, a little overweight, with a round face and light hair.

"You the girl who was assaulted?" the cop asked her, glancing once to Cameron, who gestured to her from where he leaned against the file cabinet.

"Julie…" Cameron started, and he glanced to Naomi and over her head to Dean, whom she saw in the doorway. Of course that was all he knew, and barely. At least she hadn't lied about her last name.

"Parker, Julie Parker," she spat out.

"So how about you tell me what happened here?" the cop said, still standing, appearing as if this was about to be a long night.

Then Naomi realized, as he pulled out a notepad and clicked a pen, that this was about to really become official —and that was something she couldn't have.

Chapter Seven

J ulie's nose wasn't broken, but it was swollen to almost double and impossible to breathe through, from what he could tell. It had to hurt like hell. He couldn't believe she wore contact lenses, but he'd known something was up from the way she'd been blinking furiously, her eyes watering. She'd asked the paramedic who'd shown up after the cop to remove them.

There seemed to be a lot about her that he hadn't realized. Even though she'd argued, said she was fine, and tried to tell everyone all she wanted was to go home, that wasn't happening at this point, considering they were now walking into the Casper police station.

"Look, I just want to go home. I'm tired, I hurt…" she said again, really pressing the issue.

"You need to sit down and make a statement," the cop said. He wasn't gentle, and Cameron followed, noting her balance was a little off as she stumbled in the ridiculously high heels she was in. It was lost on him how women could even walk in such things. It wasn't even ergonomically feasible, if he thought about it. Considering what it did to their bodies, their spines, their feet, all to make those mile-long legs look, what, hotter? Yeah, and hers looked incredible. *Down, boy!*

"Unfortunately, I forgot my glasses," she said, and he wondered for a moment whether she'd meant to say it out loud. "I can't see to write."

No, it was an excuse.

"Give the statement, and then I'll drive you home," Cameron said. "Don't think you need glasses for the cop to write it for you." He noted the darkening under those blue eyes from her nose hitting that door frame. It really had done a number on her face.

"I would rather not give a statement. I don't want to get involved. I just want to go home and put this night behind me." She was adamant, and he couldn't help leaning down on the desk, closer, trying to figure out what craziness was going through her head.

"You would rather a scumbag get another shot at assault, rape, and maybe something worse? What the fuck is it with you women who'd let a guy walk just to…" He was at a loss, and her face paled. "Explain to me why," he said. "He hurt you, you press charges. I'm pressing charges." He pushed away, and the cop was looking at him. Cameron wasn't sure what his expression said. *See, she's trouble. I don't care. Seen this before. Maybe in some way she deserved it?*

"You saw the assault," the cop said to Cameron. "We have your statement. We don't need her to press charges. It doesn't work that way. The scumbag is in back in a cell, and the prosecutor's been notified. She'll be compelled to testify and treated as hostile. It all comes down to making it easy or harder. I don't give a crap."

Cameron noticed the way he took her in, every inch of her, from the way she was dressed, to her face, and he grunted as if his mind was made up. It said everything.

"You know him," the cop said. It wasn't a question, and he didn't look up. For a minute, Cameron wasn't sure who he was talking to until he leveled his hard, unforgiving gaze on his waitress.

"I don't know him. I was working, and what right does that give him in any way to touch me?" Now she sounded pissed, and the cop leaned back, rested his pen on the desk. Cameron was pretty sure he could see what he was thinking.

"You proposition him, maybe work for him? You a hooker?"

He couldn't believe the cop had said that. "Hey, just a second here. She's one of my waitresses, just started. I don't know what you're insinuating, but I don't run that kind of place," he said, and he took in Julie, quiet now and slouching again, pulling at the edge of his coat to hide.

"Really? A strip club with women parading around half naked, and you think they're not asking for it, aren't putting something out on the side for a bigger tip? Is that what went down, a disagreement of some kind?"

A hand touched his arm when he stepped forward, ready to grab that cop. It had been instinctive, and it took him a second to realize it was Julie. A nice touch, and it gave him a second to think about the trouble he could have been in.

"Naomi!" he heard someone call out, frantic, and he noticed a very pretty woman with dark hair and blue eyes. A man was behind her, dark haired, clean cut, and both were moving toward Julie. "Oh, good grief, what happened? Who did this? You should have listened to me. I knew this was such a bad idea and you'd be walking into something, drowning, being way over your head. You put yourself in a situation that could have been really bad, and look."

"Taz, stop, seriously. I'm fine. Why are you here? Jerry…" She stopped talking, her voice nasal. Why had they called her Naomi? "This is my boss, Cameron." She lifted her hand, and the man held his hand out.

"Jerry O'Rourke, and this is my wife, Taz," he said. He was professional, polished, a man of means—not something he'd miss.

"Cameron Donnelly." He shook his hand.

"Taz, it's not broken," Julie said. "I'm fine."

"You're not fine. What happened?" Whoever this Taz was, she was furious, staring down at his waitress

"Guy grabbed me. He was trying to…" She cleared her throat. "Cameron stopped him."

He noted how quiet Taz had become, staring down in horror at Julie, whom she'd called Naomi. Another secret? He wondered. Jerry was taking in the cop and then Cameron. His face said how unhappy he was.

"Taz is right, Naomi. You got in over your head. There's no way your father would be okay with any of this. You know that." Jerry turned to him. "You stopped this?"

"Yup, and just to be clear, that guy would have had her out the door, and if he'd just raped her, she'd have gotten off easy. Now how about somebody fill me in on who you really are and why you told me your name is Julie, yet these folks here are calling you Naomi?"

Both Jerry and Taz gave all their attention to her. She was staring up at him with blue eyes that were bloodshot, eyes which held something. Secrets and lies, those he was familiar with.

"Julie is my middle name, and Taz is my sister."

Chapter Eight

Explaining was something she didn't do. She was the curious one, always asking questions, but as she sat in her parents' kitchen now in a high-back chair pulled away from the table, her mother held a warm washcloth out to her. Her dad, though blurred, was standing, facing her, his thick hair in need of a cut and graying more and more, his long-sleeved shirt rolled up to his elbows, and his hands fisted at his sides. Chris, her sister Ivy's boyfriend, was also there, tall, dark haired, totally ripped, and staring at her as if she'd done something totally stupid, from what she could make out—or maybe that was what she believed everyone was thinking.

The back door clattered.

"Okay, let me have a look." Ivy, the maternity ward nurse, walked in, her dark hair hiked high in a ponytail. She was wearing blue jeans and a Redskins jersey, and they both appeared baggy from the noticeable pounds her sister had lost, having taken up jogging and the gym. She stopped in front of Naomi and stuck a thermometer in her ear.

"I hurt my nose," she said. "I don't have a fever." Even she wanted to wince at the nasal sound of her voice. It was painful, and now Scarlett, her brat of a younger eighteen-year-old sister, leaned in, taking in Naomi. It was the first time she'd seen her sister, who was the drama queen of the family, always wanting center stage, quiet.

"Don't talk anymore," Ivy said. "It's painful to hear." The thermometer beeped, and she pulled it out. "Normal."

Naomi was about to say 'Told you,' but she doubted from the way everyone was standing over her that that would be the wisest course right now. She was glad she couldn't see clearly.

"So a guy did this to you." Her dad spoke so low, but there was no mistaking it. Nothing in his voice was soft.

"Yes, it was…" She closed her mouth to swallow, because she still couldn't breathe through her nose, and her throat was starting to hurt. Ivy was looking at her nose, which she knew was swollen, closely and poking at an especially sore spot. "Ouch, stop touching! That hurts."

"I don't think it's broken, but you said a paramedic looked at it, not a doctor."

Now Mason appeared in her face, leaning in. She was the baby of the family, at seventeen, with hair a muted golden color Naomi hadn't seen on her before. "I bet it's broken," she said. "Look at the size of that. Remember Clive Westmore taking that baseball to his nose? It sort of looked like that, and his was definitely broken." Then Mason touched her hair, which was pinned back with strands hanging everywhere, a mess, and tangled. She held a long lock of blond up as if studying the color. "So who colored your hair?"

"Me," she said, wishing everyone would stop examining her. It was damn uncomfortable.

"Nice job," Mason said, still inspecting it.

This was like a bad nightmare as she heard the door clatter again, hearing footsteps. Keys landed on the table, hers, and she didn't have to look over to know Jerry had now joined them after going back to the bar with Cameron and retrieving her car, her things. How bad was this night going to get?

"You got all Naomi's things?" Taz asked. Thankfully Ivy was still standing in front of her, blocking her view of the inquisition team waiting to, what, rake a grown woman over the coals? Ground her? The thought made her want to laugh. She was twenty-four. Why was this even up for discussion?

"Purse, coat. Wasn't sure that was all," Jerry said as if she weren't there. "I had a chat with a few waitresses and the barkeeper, then had a look around."

"Help me out here, Naomi," her dad said. "Just so that I understand everything, you're working in a strip club, doing what, again?"

She wondered whether it was a question. Her mother still hadn't said a word, and she wished someone would give her a sweater, a blanket, anything to cover up what little she had on. She was embarrassed. She felt naked, sitting in the chair before her family, everyone seeing her at her most vulnerable.

"It's a bar. There are strippers. I'm working on a story, undercover. I'm a waitress, not taking my clothes off. There's a difference," she said as if this made everything all right. She coughed, feeling the dried blood in her nose, and it hurt. She wanted something for the pain, and maybe Ivy read her mind, as she held up a bottle of Advil and dumped some in her hand.

"Scarlett, get Naomi a glass of water. Here's two. They're extra strength, so they should take the edge off."

She took the pills from her hand and dumped them in her mouth, then swallowed the water from the glass Scarlett handed to her. "Thank you," she said as Ivy took the glass.

"You're crazy in over your head, Naomi," Taz said. "I can't believe after hearing about this yesterday how bad an idea it was. I had a feeling something would go wrong, that we should have stopped this crazy idea of yours."

"You knew about this and said nothing to us, Taz?" Her mother, Susan Parker, sounded genuinely hurt, accusing, and Naomi had to turn her head to see her. Ivy handed her her glasses, and she slid them on, holding them up and away from her nose. Now she could see, and she wished she couldn't. The hurt and shock on her family's faces was almost too much.

Ivy stepped away, and she could now see her dad's face clearly. It was an expression that said she'd really fucked up. He'd become quiet, and she didn't have a clue what he was thinking of her. This was a father she'd seen like this only a time or two, the kind of man she didn't cross.

"Last night, when we saw Naomi pull in after she missed dinner, I wanted to say hi and walked in on her in this." She gestured to her state of dress. "She told us—"

"Taz" was all Jerry said. It sounded like a warning. Even his expression was something Naomi wasn't familiar with. "It seems your daughter is running a story on Cameron Donnelly and is working undercover as a waitress in his bar to get close to him. Isn't that what you said?" Jerry was looking directly at her. and she could feel how quiet the room was. Everyone was watching, waiting for her to say…what?

"Who's Cameron Donnelly?" Chris asked. It was the million-dollar question. Of course he wouldn't know, being from Kansas City. He'd never have heard of the scandal, the investigations that had never borne any fruit. The man had found loopholes, cheated those around him, and destroyed a woman's life.

"A very bad man," she said. Everyone looked at her, and no one said anything else.

Chapter Nine

She'd taken a bath and was in her nightshirt with a blanket over her legs as she relaxed on her sofa.

"Here, chamomile." Ivy was holding a steaming mug. "It'll help relax you."

Her door opened, and Chris walked in, wearing work boots, blue jeans, and a T-shirt of some sports team she couldn't make out. He was so damn attractive, yet he only had eyes for Ivy as he walked over, taking her in, his hands sliding over the small of her back and resting on her ass. Possessive, close, so in love.

"Everything good here?" he said.

Naomi was so done talking. She lifted the mug and blew, and the steam fogged up her glasses. Good, she couldn't see anymore.

When she pulled it away and her glasses unfogged, Chris was still watching her, and Ivy was standing over her like a mother hen. It wasn't lost on her how furious her mother had been, too. No, actually, it was way past that, considering she wasn't over here fussing or even yelling, telling her over and over how badly she'd screwed up. It hurt.

"Jerry just got off the phone with the Casper cop handling the case," Chris said. "Assault only. They're apparently not proceeding with attempted rape, and the guy is getting a slap on the wrist for the assault charge and will be out on bail." He stared down at Ivy, maybe waiting for her to do or say something.

"I froze," Naomi said.

She hadn't planned on saying that, and both Chris and Ivy were staring at her as if she'd said she was packing up and going to the moon. She rested the hot mug on the homemade carved coffee table and placed her hands in her lap, feeling so many things now that she'd had a few hours away from everyone either yelling at her or questioning her and then looking at her as if she were this huge disappointment, making her feel horrible.

"I didn't expect that to happen. He was walking past me, and the hallway was dark, and he put his hand on me. I don't even remember what I said to him, because I was shocked, and then he had me against the wall. I just remember there was no one around, and I tried to scream. It was the one thing I think I tried to do. Then he covered my mouth, and he was moving to the door. I remember him saying something but not the exact words. It was his meaning, as if he believed he had every right to touch me like he did because of how I was dressed, who I was, and where we were. He was going to rape me. I know that now even though I didn't really understand it then, all because I froze." Her hand slid up over her chest to cover herself.

"It happens, Naomi…" Ivy said rather calmly.

"Never have I had a man think he could just do whatever he wanted to me as if I was nothing and he had every right. Working in that bar, dressed as I was, he made me feel cheap, worthless, as if I was without any meaning. No one has ever made me feel as if I didn't matter. Those guys came in from that oilfield in the middle of the day, looking to get drunk and lucky. They thought they had every right to touch me, slide their hands under my skirt, pinch my ass, touch my breasts, and I took it, but when that guy…" Her chest tightened, and her eyes burned. She couldn't talk anymore, and she lifted the blanket, pulling it up in front of her.

"He was stronger than you," Chris said. "Men are stronger, it's a fact, and he used that power to his advantage. That's a crime. He didn't have any right to do what he did. He got a slap on the wrist for something he should be doing hard time for." He sounded so mad, but it didn't make her feel any better. He was standing over her, and for the first time she realized he was a part of this family. She hadn't really picked up on that before as he and Ivy had grown closer, now living together in her cabin. And her dad was okay with it? It had just sort of evolved, and they were so perfect for each other. She'd never have thought.

Naomi just stared up at him and then her sister. "So why do I feel as if I'm the one who did something wrong?"

"Victims usually do, no matter how irrational it is. I've seen it time and again in the hospital," Ivy said.

Chris had a hard set to his face and seemed to be considering something. "I'm not a woman, so I can't understand how you feel, but I can only imagine a lot of it had to do with you not knowing how to defend yourself and having no idea what to do if a man grabbed you. Each and every one of you girls needs to know how to defend yourself. It needs to be drilled into you so that it's instinct." He sounded almost mad again, and Ivy was looking at him now as if ready to argue. She was no pushover, and as strong willed as he was, it was almost difficult at times to be standing there when she said no to him or disagreed or argued with him.

"Naomi not knowing how to defend herself has nothing to do with the fact that a man tried to rape her," she snapped, her hands on her hips, so close to Chris.

"That's not what I said, so don't put words in my mouth. Naomi walked into something that was dangerous and foolish and put herself in harm's way without having a contingency plan for if some redneck decided to force himself on her. She couldn't protect herself, none of you girls could, and this should be enough of a wakeup that every one of you will learn how to protect yourself. Even the army trains its recruits better."

"So you're saying the army protects its women, yet said women who know how to protect themselves are raped by the same military men who've trained them—"

"Enough." He cut her off, appearing frustrated.

Naomi wasn't sure what to make of the disagreement that was happening over, what, her or what had happened? Had they forgotten she was there?

"That's not what I'm saying, and that's a whole other issue altogether. What I'm saying is at least the army trains women to protect themselves. It doesn't always work. There are always things that happen. Let's not start going down that road. We're talking about your sister!" Chris was now yelling, and she could see how upset he was. For a minute, she thought it really was just the two of them together and they'd forgotten about her. It was uncomfortable, and she glanced over to the door, wondering whether she could just slip out of her house.

Ivy rested her hand on her chest, which rose with fury and emotion. All of it was there between them, and Naomi was alone. She cleared her throat roughly to break the tension.

"You okay for tonight?" Ivy asked, but she didn't look her way, as she was staring up at Chris, who was now standing with his hands on his hips, inches from her. She could see so clearly now that he was all about fixing things, and he loved her sister more than she could have imagined. Chris said nothing else other than wiping his face. She could hear the scrape of whiskers as he seemed to pull himself together.

"I'm fine," Naomi said. "You don't need to stay. Are Taz and Jerry staying over?" She thought they would've left that morning or at least tonight.

"No, they're staying a few days in her cabin, or tonight, at least. Jerry isn't happy about the bar, and I heard him with Dad and Chris talking about what happened as I came over to check on you." Ivy was looking to Chris as if he knew more.

It was worse than she imagined, and she went to place her hand to her face before remembering the swelling. She pulled her hand away and fisted it, feeling the ache pound again.

"I still don't understand who this guy is that you'd place yourself directly in danger in this way," Chris said. "It's a bad place. The guys who frequent that kind of place flood in from the oilfield, and I know the type. So does your dad. These are the kind who work hard in an industry that leaves everything civilized behind. What happened today could happen again. Not likely you'll be going back there, but worse, Naomi, this guy's walking after what he did. That should be a warning to you, at least. I'm sure your dad's going down there. Heard Jerry talking, too. They wanted to have a sit-down with the cop, maybe the DA, and for sure the owner of that strip club."

That had her sitting up straighter, because a talk like that couldn't happen. "Dad's doing what?" She put her feet to the floor, dropping the blanket. "He can't. They can't."

"Unfortunately, Naomi, this time I agree with Dad and Jerry. They can, and they should. Drop this story. Find something safer." Her sister stepped around the table, leaned down, and touched her shoulder before stepping away.

"No, I'm not dropping it. This is my story. I'm really good at what I do, and I can't have my dad and my sister's husband racing in to solve my problems or whatever it is they're planning to do. What are they doing?" She was panicked, thinking Cameron would know what she was up to and learn that everything about her was a lie. She'd lose the story and any chance her paper would let her do a job like this ever again—and she'd never get close to Cameron again. She'd be blacklisted.

"You would seriously go back after what happened?" Chris was shaking his head, and she didn't care what he thought at this point. She wanted to preserve her dignity and lie. When she said nothing, he made a rude noise. "I may not have a say in what you do, but your dad and Jerry have already left. If I did, you wouldn't be setting one foot into a place like that, where you don't belong."

Whatever it was that passed between her sister and Chris, she didn't expect what came next.

"I get it, Naomi, I really do," Ivy said, "and maybe I'm secretly cheering you on for what you have the balls to do, the balls to expose, but if you're going to go back to that kind of place, make sure there isn't a next time. Chris is right about one thing: You better make sure you know how to defend yourself."

Chapter Ten

"You heard from Julie?" Cameron asked as he strode into the tiny back office, which had not even a small window. Aside from Dean, Joe was there as well, his hair neat and tidy, wearing a white T-shirt and dark blue jeans. It was at that second that Cameron realized he'd just stepped into the middle of something heated. They both were quiet now as he took another minute to realize how much this place didn't suit him. The thought took his mood to something dark and unpleasant.

"No." Dean shook his head. "But we should have a discussion about her and why she's not fit for a place like this, and whether it's even a good idea she comes back." He tapped the desk with his knuckles and then gestured to Joe. "And about other things that have gone on right under your nose here."

Cameron wasn't sure what passed between the men, but the bartender stood up and moved away, taking in Dean again. Another heavy look passed between them.

"Can't see her coming back after what happened," Joe said. "She should be scared and hopefully has come to her senses. Pegged her as green the moment she showed up yesterday. No matter how she looked, she wasn't meant to fit in a place like this—and please consider those names I left you for an extra bouncer. That would have prevented what happened to Julie." Then he slid his hand over the door jamb, taking in Cameron. It was odd, the way he seemed to be trying to figure him out. Joe was a hard man to read, either good or bad. He didn't have a clue.

He turned back to Dean, who had an odd look on his face. "What was that about?" he asked, sitting on the edge of the desk, his arms crossed, wondering what kind of problems would be coming up next for him.

"Doing what you wanted, what you should have done," Dean said. "Been talking with everyone here and finding out who else knew what Pete was up to, everyone and anyone. Clients were coming in, asking for drugs, and he was selling them here right under your nose. Someone had to see. Someone had to know."

"And?" he asked, wondering who'd be fired next. Maybe closing the doors on this place would be the better idea.

"Just as expected, no one saw anything or had any idea he was doing something illegal. So far I've spoken to the bartender, four of the dancers, and three waitresses, and every one of them has hinted that it had to be isolated and they had no idea he was selling drugs. But every one of them is lying, I tell you. It's what happens, the way of the street: Don't talk, and definitely don't let on that you know something or saw anything."

He couldn't believe the headache he had with this place, even though it had turned into one of the biggest cash cows he'd had. Maybe that was why he hadn't sold it. He should reconsider. "The cameras?" he asked.

His brother smiled, a dark hint of something that

seemed to say *You should know better* filling his expression. "Tonight, after everyone's gone, I'll have them installed everywhere. No more blind spots, and no more waitresses getting hurt. No more anyone doing anything illegal—drugs, sex, nothing. And since we're on the subject of hot babes and sex, mind if I give you some advice about your recent hire?" Dean leaned back in his chair, and it squeaked. He had the expression of a man who could see everyone for who and what they were. Maybe that was why Cameron liked having him around.

"What?"

"Get rid of her, Julie, if she comes back, and hopefully she won't. Today should have shown her that she was lucky and doesn't fit here. Cut her a check, add in a few hundred for her trouble and injuries, and then send her on her way," he said with a flick of his hand just as there was a tap on the open door, where Joe appeared again.

"Mr. Donnelly, there's two men out front asking for you. One says he's Julie's father, and the other is the guy who came back with you to get her car and things. What do you want me to tell them?"

Cameron glanced to his brother, wondering what they possibly wanted, and then back to Joe. "Nothing. I'll come out and deal with them." *Personally,* he thought, *and find out whether this is a shakedown or a message.*

"You want me to tag along, see what they want?" Dean said.

He shook his head. That was the last thing he wanted, considering he was more than a little curious about the painted-up waitress who seemed to have a different story than she'd depicted. "No, I got this," he said and then walked out and down the darkened hallway, taking in the spot by the exit where Julie had hit her face and been manhandled by that drunken rig worker.

He kept on to the door as the music pounded, picking up in volume the closer he got, blasting as he opened it and saw that the bar was hopping. A naked woman was onstage, and some men were hooting and yelling, some silent and lost in her charms. By the bar were two men, one older, who would never fit in a place like this.

Jerry had his eyes on him and lifted his hand as if to flag him down. The man filled his space, confident in his skill and in what he did. The older man with him appeared uncomfortable, but at the same time, as he approached, Cameron got the impression this was a man he could easily misread.

"Cameron," Jerry said as he met him halfway, holding out his hand and shaking it. "This is Naomi's father, Robert Parker. We'd like a word with you if you have a minute."

He was a man of means, business savvy, and Cameron picked up on something else then, too. It wasn't just the way he dressed, but there was something about him. There was that name again, Naomi. The tall distinguished man, Robert, had thick hair, a mix of gray and dark, and was wearing a worn heavy jacket over faded jeans. A working man, he could see it, but different from the type who frequented the bar. His hands were big and callused as he extended one in a firm shake.

Robert had been giving Cameron all his attention, but he'd yet to say a word as he took in this place, all of it. Cameron didn't have a clue what the man was thinking. He appeared uncomfortable in an odd sort of way as a redheaded waitress started toward him from across the bar before Cameron shook his head. She was in a tight tank, breasts half hanging out, her skirt so short and appearing painted on. She turned and went the other way.

"So you're the man who put my daughter in danger" was all Robert said.

Cameron glanced to Jerry, who was giving him nothing and everything at the same time. "I'm not sure what Julie told you, or is it Naomi? Really would like to know what's going on. She was desperate for a job, or so she said, but I'm trying to figure out how this daughter of yours is so desperate to work in a place like this when she comes from a family who evidently cares for her. But then, I learned long ago things quite often aren't as they appear," he said, taking in the two men. For the life of him, he didn't know what to make of them or of Julie. Why was she so hard up that she had to work in a place like this?

"She said she was desperate for a job?" Robert said. Jerry appeared uncomfortable, and it didn't take Cameron all of two seconds to figure out he knew something. Now he was starting to wonder what the story really was.

"She did, but I take it she isn't. I would appreciate someone filling me in on the real story. How about her name to start? Is it Naomi, not Julie?"

Neither said anything, but they exchanged a look. The way Robert glanced around then, pissed off, had Cameron's temper, which didn't flare often, spiking.

"I have five daughters," Robert said. "Love my girls. Two are married." He shook his head, maybe in disbelief or frustration. "Regardless, I can't understand the kind of man who lets women who work for him be put in danger, be pawed at. Maybe I don't get this, the need and why a man would own a place like this. Some say it's okay, men need to blow off steam, relax, let loose, and the girls here are doing what they're doing because they're just those types of girls—but not my daughter, not ever. As a father, I'm not okay with this. She won't be coming back. If I'd known..." He stopped himself from saying more, shaking his head and taking in Jerry before turning back to Cameron with a look on his face that was close to hate and disgust. It implied a warning, he was sure, not to get close to his daughter again. Just as well, but at the same time he needed to know she was okay.

"Fair enough. How is she?" he asked.

Jerry said, "Shaken up, bruised. The scope of what happened probably hasn't hit her."

It answered a lot and at the same time left him with more questions. "I'll cut her a check and something to at least cover her medical bills, something at least for the injury."

Robert shook his head. "No, keep your money," he said as if it were worthless or tainted.

"No. She worked here a day, and she'll be paid for that whether she cashes the check or not. Leave the address and I'll send it out."

Jerry reached in his jacket and pulled out a card. He gestured to the bartender for a pen and then scribbled something on the back. With two fingers, he passed it over to Cameron. He noted the name and then the logo of the security firm in Denver. He had written down a rural address outside Kaycee. "Thanks for seeing us," Jerry added, ready to leave.

"Hey, hold up a second," Cameron said. "You're in security?"

Jerry just looked at him, and for a moment Cameron wondered if he'd answer him. "I am."

"What kind of security do you do? I see by this card you're based in Denver, but you're here…" He let the question hang as Jerry nodded.

"Visiting Taz and her family, but yes, I have a firm over in Denver and in Montana, mostly personal bodyguards, full-fledged security for businesses, homes, and those who need it. Monitoring, too, and everything in between. Thanks for your time, Cameron." It was a dismissal, and he was ready to leave again.

"Wait a second," Cameron said, stopping them. "Wondering if you'd consider something. I have a situation, and if you'd be open to discussing some details, I'd like to hire you."

Chapter Eleven

She didn't think it was possible for her nose to hurt more than it had the day before. In fact, it wasn't just her nose. It felt as if her entire face had been hit by a Mack truck as she made her way down the steps from bed, the sun bright, her glasses resting on top of her head because of the swelling and the fact that anything touching her nose hurt.

She made her way into the bathroom, not hearing a sound outside, which was unusual. When she saw her face in the mirror, the image staring back at her was black and blue and swelling, a hideous image she couldn't show to anyone. No wonder she hurt the way she did, so she opened the medicine cabinet above the sink and pulled out a bottle of Advil. She swallowed straight from the tap, and though she snorted a bit, she was careful not to touch her nose, happy at least she could breathe a little out of it today.

With Cameron, Jerry, Taz, her father, and even Chris, let alone her mom, who still hadn't said two words to her, she thought she'd do better to hide out for the day. Then her cell phone rang. It was coming from her purse, sitting on her small round kitchen table along with the coat Jerry had retrieved. That was another issue she needed to address. What exactly had Jerry and Cameron discussed? She pulled out her phone and saw Flory's name, then realized she hadn't checked in the day before.

"Hi, Flory. Sorry I didn't call—"

"You got hurt!" Flory snapped, cutting her off.

She winced, but that only added to the pounding in her face. "Who told you?" she asked as she heard a *Tsk* over the phone.

"Came over the wire. Heard of an incident in Casper, then saw the name of the bar, the assault, and figured it out. So what the hell happened, and are you okay?"

"I'm fine, really, just got caught off guard by some drunk who grabbed me and…"

"Tried to hurt you," she said, cutting her off again. "Don't sugarcoat this. You tell me everything or this is over for you and you're back at a desk forever. I knew I shouldn't have humored you and allowed you to walk into something there was no way you were ready to handle."

Okay, that wasn't fair, and she resented the implication. "Flory, he was drunk, bigger and stronger, and it could have happened to anyone, but Cameron stopped him from taking me out the door." Her throat closed up as she started shaking. Again the implication of what he was going to do to her really hit home, and she had to sit down.

"Well, thank goodness for that. I heard you were injured?"

"My nose, face. I hit the wall. Right now my face is black and blue and hurts like hell, but at least I can breathe out of my nose this morning. But I'm okay. They're charging him with…" Nothing, as she remembered what

Chris had said the night before. She felt her shoulders sag as the feeling of being worthless hit again.

"Aggravated assault, no jail time, yet I understand he would have raped you."

There it was.

"Yeah, can't believe it. I didn't expect that, even though last night I was of the mind to just let him walk because of the story. I wasn't thinking it through, and you know what really pisses me off is that cop, the way he looked at me and what I was wearing, some of the things he said to me. He really believed I brought this on, as if it was my fault. Maybe that should be the story," she said, wishing something would be done and said to protect women more.

"Maybe it should, but you'd be hard pressed to get anyone to listen—especially men, not that it's not a good story. It's overdue. It's just I've worked it so many times, so many countries, and I've had too many men say, 'Oh, you and the girls. It's always something about girls, women. It's old news. People don't care anymore.' And you know what I realized? They were right. Sex trade workers, strippers, waitresses in nightclubs, they're targets and are victimized, but those crimes are the least reported, the least convicted. It's not right, but it is the way. You sure you're okay? This is the kind of thing that can really mess with you. Listen, take a few days, get some rest."

She heard typing or something in the background. "I need to call Cameron at least, talk to him and let him know I'm not coming in today." At least she now was one step closer to him. At least one good thing had come out of her assault.

"Maybe you're not understanding, so I'm going to be clear. The story's dead, not happening. Take a few days, regroup, get your head together, and we'll talk. I'm thinking of putting you on Bernie's column."

She wanted to scream when she heard it. "Bernie has the community opinion stuck at the back of the paper, which no one reads."

"And there's no way you're going back to Casper, to that bar. Not happening, no way. Leave it be, Naomi. The paper doesn't want to take the chance of you getting seriously hurt. An exposé is one thing done by a big-name paper, a reporter who's made for undercover and digging. You're young, and—"

"I can do this. Just give me a chance. Flory, you of all people should understand what it means to expose the truth, get the guy who's lied and cheated and gotten to the position he has because of who he is."

"That's exactly why I'm shutting this down, because this isn't the story for you. This was a human interest story about the personal side of this guy, and it's now off the rails with you getting hurt. I do know what it means to expose the truth and find a story and dig up sources and evidence of something that matters, but you'll get in over your head and get buried, and then, even when you think you've done it right, you'll have the rug pulled out from under you because of a source who's lied or facts that were altered, steering everyone from the true story. Listen, Naomi, Cameron Donnelly is a big guy, and I told you before the CEO only gave a provisional okay."

"What if I can meet with Cameron and get the story without working there?" How the hell she was going to do that, she hadn't a clue.

There was silence and then munching. Hallelujah for those Doritos; it meant she was thinking, a good thing. "Meeting, not working, in what way?" she asked as she chewed again.

"I mean, Cameron was the one who saved me, who took me to the police station. I've got an in now because of this." She was really working it. "He was the one who took the guy down and was ready to throw the book at him." And he'd given her his coat and hadn't made an excuse or had one of his employees hang with her or tag along to the station.

Silence again. This was good.

"You think you can get Cameron to see you outside of Casper?" she asked, and Naomi for the first time felt as if she was back in the game.

"I do. Just give me a shot, and this time, if it doesn't work, you win. I walk away from this, and…" She swallowed, just thinking of what she wasn't about to give up.

"You'll take the column?" Flory asked, chewing again. She heard the foil of the Doritos bag in the background.

"I'll take the column."

"Deal, but hear me on this. Under no circumstances are you to waitress again in that bar," she said.

Naomi wanted to jump up and down, feeling the victory. "You got it."

Chapter Twelve

Her mother was behind the house in the garden, walking through a row of peas. She lifted a big silver bowl full of greens and lettuce.

Naomi hesitated for a second when her mom's all-knowing gaze landed on her. "Hi, Mom," she said. How lame was that? She winced.

Susan Parker had on shorts that stopped at her knees and a faded green sleeveless blouse. Her graying hair was tied back in a ponytail. The smile she always had for her kids left her face. "So how are you feeling today? Didn't see you at breakfast," she said. The fact that she hadn't come over and checked on her last night or even this morning let her know that her mom was more upset than she'd originally thought.

"Good," she lied, and her mom made a face, most likely at the horrific sight staring back at her.

"It looks worse." Her mom touched her chin, turned her head, and winced. "Good Lord, Naomi, what were you thinking?"

She wondered if that was something all mothers said.

"I was thinking about my job. I didn't ask for the guy to do this to me, Mom. It's not my fault," she added even though part of her couldn't help feeling shamed and worse, as if she'd somehow brought some of this on herself. She knew it wasn't rational.

"Naomi, I thought I raised you girls better. Your dad and I can't believe what you put yourself in, and don't say again it was because of your job. You've never taken something like this on. I would have thought this kind of thing was outside the scope of the reporting you were doing. I know you've always been the curious one, always asking questions, so it never surprised me that you got into the news business. You said you'd be a journalist, and I believed you would, but, Naomi, a strip club and dressing as…" Her mom was making her feel even worse, and she wanted to turn tail and slip on back to her cabin and shut the door.

"Sorry to disappoint you, Mom, but this is who I am, and I'm not going to change to make you feel better, or Dad." She took a step back, and her mom frowned.

"Because I voice my opinion? Don't disrespect me and walk away, Naomi. I'm upset with you because you put yourself in danger. As your mother, I have that right. I don't think you have any idea what could have happened. When you came home yesterday with Taz, hurt and dressed up as if playing a part, I didn't recognize you." There was sadness and fear and something else in her mom's eyes, something she'd seen only once before when her eldest sister had up and left town with that rodeo cowboy who'd dumped her years later with five kids on the side of the road in Montana. She didn't want to be responsible for putting any more hurt there, but at the same time, why didn't her family get the fact that this was going to happen? This was a story that needed to be told.

"I do know what could have happened, but all the same, Mom, it didn't. I'm not about to live in fear of what could have happened." Even though her mind kept dragging her back to relive the events over and over, reliving his touch, the stench of liquor and sweat. All of it hit her as she felt her heartbeat kick up, sliding into anxiety that skipped over to panic and came with a cold sweat. She'd never before felt it, but she'd heard others talk of it. Now she knew. She squeezed the shirt at her chest.

"Good, then at least learn from it, Naomi. I don't think you understand what it can do to a woman to be raped. It's a violation that can haunt you for the rest of your life and leave you unable to have a healthy relationship with any man. It happened to a friend of mine when I was young, from school, one wrong choice, something teenagers do. She got into a car she shouldn't have, and..." Her mom stopped talking. Her expression was frozen before she lifted her hand. "Anyway, it was a long time ago, before I married your father. It was rough on her, and she was never the same after that."

She wanted to know more. "You've never talked about this, a friend?" she said.

Her mom looked away, her eyes filled with heavy thoughts and something else, too. "Not something I want to rehash, but I'm telling you so you understand that a woman has to be careful and aware. It can happen anywhere, but putting yourself into a position where you're walking right into danger isn't smart. Dressed as you were, in a bar frequented by the kind of men who are working in an industry where they work hard and play hard, living on the edge... Those are not gentlemen, and they have no respect for women. Not a great combination. Why Cameron Donnelly? Why the interest?"

"Because of who he is," she said, not getting why her mom wasn't screaming at her to nail his ass.

"And who is he and what has he done that has you needing to put yourself in harm's way like this?"

For the first time, she was at a loss for words. "Mom, don't you remember the article that came out, the local news? He's horrible. He's done every terrible thing, making money off the most vulnerable, screwing Americans over, cheating. He has foreign ties—and then there's the women."

Her mom was still looking at her, and she couldn't understand how she didn't get that Cameron was about making money off the backs of others, finding loopholes in Wyoming state laws and skimming money off the top, all the while creating a haven for foreign money. Then she looked away.

"You know what, Naomi? I don't pay much attention to all that, and at times I don't believe everything that's out there. If I remember correctly, it was conjecture and a lot of gossip, but there was no proof of anything. If he is what you say, they'll find it or not, but there's something more important: you and your wellbeing."

Her mom stepped closer, slipping the bowl to her side, holding it with one arm, her hand over Naomi's shoulder. She held her face, her chin, so gently, the way a mother does to comfort. "I don't want what happened to my best friend to happen to any of you." She stepped back, as a car was coming. They could hear anyone in the distance on the road, the gravel, the dust, which added to the show.

"You expecting someone?" Naomi asked, not sure why her heart was hammering and her hands were sweating. She didn't recognize the car.

"No," her mom said as they started around the house, seeing Taz and Jerry coming out of their cabin, but no one else was around. Scarlett and Mason were at school, Ivy most likely at work, her car gone, and Chris and her dad too had gone, off working on some job. As the car pulled closer, she noticed it was a German import, a newer black BMW. It stopped in front of Taz's cabin, beside Jerry's Mercedes, and the man who stepped out had her stomach dropping to her feet.

"Oh shit," she said as she stared at the tall, very good-looking man who walked over to Jerry, shook his hand, and exchanged words with him. As he looked over to her, everything changed. He slid off his sunglasses and tucked them in his shirtfront. Cameron Donnelly was here, and she was so screwed.

Chapter Thirteen

The town of Kaycee was a smaller part of Wyoming. Cameron could honestly say he'd been up this way only a time or two. He'd been wondering a whole lot since even before Robert and Jerry had stepped into his bar. In the mostly quiet ride back from the police station, he'd picked up more questions than answers from Jerry, but he'd put out the offer to oversee the security and work with Dean to identify any problems, mainly vetting all the people working for him. He hadn't shared his plans to start unloading some of these businesses that he'd inadvertently acquired, the type that came with problems, the kind of surprises he would live a longer and happier life without.

Jerry hadn't committed but had said he'd get back to him. However, he needed to pay Julie, a.k.a. Naomi, a visit and maybe get some answers to the more nagging questions. That was one reason he found himself driving out to the home address on the back of the card. He stood there, taking in the large property, which was mostly flat, pristine, with grassy swells here and there. The main building was a neat and tidy smaller ranch house, and three identical cottages lay not fifty feet from it.

Everything appeared well built, with more of a homey welcoming feeling than he'd have expected. It was the kind of place that said family, which only added to his feeling that something was really off. He parked beside a nice back Mercedes in front of the first cottage. Someone had money, and as he stepped out, he didn't miss the older compact of his waitress, the car Jerry had stopped by to pick up just the day earlier, over by the last cottage—a cottage that was far from rundown or screaming of hardship.

"Didn't expect you," Jerry called out, getting his attention as he walked out of the first cottage. The woman he'd met that night at the police station was beside him. What was her name? He had to think, as women's names didn't stick with him anymore. Maybe it was the fact that many weren't worth the trouble. He realized Jerry and Julie's sister appeared far from happy to see him. That kind of unwelcome greeting wasn't a stranger to him.

"Sorry, wanted to get some answers and deliver a check." He held out his hand to Jerry, shook it, and then picked up two women in the distance walking from behind the house. One was Julie, her face a mess, with an older woman, and both appeared far from hard times. They were both coming his way. "I was hoping to have a moment with you to talk more about working for me, hopefully share some details and enough about why, if you have time, to convince you." He took in the women getting closer.

Jerry was now holding his wife's hand. He glanced down to her once. "Well, the thing is, Cameron, we don't live here, and as I said last night, we're only down visiting but really need to head back to Denver."

Not what he wanted to hear as Julie approached, her face a mix of panic and something else.

"Cameron," she said. "I'm sorry. Didn't know you were coming out here. Why are you here?" She was looking to Jerry and his wife—Taz. The older woman held out her hand. He was thinking she was her mother, by the resemblance.

"I'm Naomi's mother, Susan Parker. You are?" she asked, and her manners weren't lost on him.

"Cameron Donnelly. Your daughter worked for me," he said, and he didn't miss the big O her mouth made. "Just so we're clear, is it Julie or Naomi?"

Everyone gave her a questioning glance. Yeah, as he thought. Even through the bruising, he could see the flush.

"As I said, Julie is my middle name," she replied. No one said anything to contradict her, but the impression he was getting screamed deception, something he was also quite familiar with.

"So how do I address you, Julie or Naomi? Which is it?" he asked again, waiting. He didn't need to look over to see how uncomfortable Jerry and Taz were. Her mother seemed to be studying him and then her daughter. He wasn't sure why.

"Naomi, please," she said. At least that was now settled.

"Great. I brought along your last check." He reached in his jacket and lifted it out, then handed it to her. "I wanted to see how you are, if you're okay."

Her long hair was tied back, and maybe it was the way she was dressed that had thrown him a bit. It wasn't the slutty dress all the ladies in his bar wore. It was faded jeans and a loose T-shirt with a baggy sweater overtop. Nothing that showed her fantastic figure. Her nose was swollen still, with a mass of bruises under her eyes. She had dark-rimmed glasses and no thick makeup. It was quite the difference.

"Just sore, but fine. Thanks for asking," she said, staring at the envelope, her face pinched and thinking.

"I can't help wondering and am just going to ask straight out, since I can't stand when things are left unsaid, but there's nothing about you that jives with the image of the hard-up lady begging me for a job. I've met your father, your brother-in-law, and now I come out here and see this, and can't help wondering, what it is you're hiding, Naomi? What is it that had you driving all the way to Casper, how many miles from where you live, to pretend to be someone you're not? If there's one thing I don't like, it's lies, deception, and this all feels like one big one. So how about we dispense with all the bullshit and niceties and you tell me what it is you really wanted and why you really came begging to work in a sleazy bar?" he said, feeling the pump of adrenaline.

She said nothing for a moment or two as Taz glanced awkwardly away. Susan was staring down at her daughter, and Naomi finally relented as if giving in.

"I'm a reporter," she said and this time met his gaze straight on. He said nothing. "Would you sit down with me and answer some questions?"

Of every possibility he'd suspected, that definitely hadn't been one of them. It took him a minute to wonder what it was she wanted from him, to fuck up his life way more than it already was? "A reporter for who?" he asked. Why now? What the hell had he done that someone was here again, sniffing around, trying to destroy his life?

"I work out of Buffalo, the *Gazette*," she said. "It's about you as a person, an article about…" She hesitated, and he had to wonder why old skeletons were being dug up again, ones that weren't even his.

"I have no comment for the press, no interest to speak with you, and I guess I can understand your reluctance now to accept a job, Jerry. You knew about this?"

Jerry didn't look happy. Even Taz appeared uncomfortable. He had his arms crossed now, holding on to something and not saying anything.

Cameron stepped back, his keys in his hand, and took one last look at this family, this place, the woman who wasn't who she'd pretended to be. He turned back to her. "If you ever show your face in one of my places of business again, I'll contact my lawyers and sue your paper for harassment," he said. Then he walked over to his car, opened the door, and took in the shock and worry on her face. No one said anything at all.

Chapter Fourteen

"Consider it one of those life lessons and walk away," Taz said. She had finished stuffing her suitcase with clothes, and Jerry was outside, loading up his Mercedes. In a matter of moments, they were going to be on the road back to Denver. Her mom hadn't made an excuse. She'd gone back into the house, saying she had things to do.

"I can't just walk away, and I still can't believe he showed up here. Why would he, and how did he know where to bring the check?" she added as Jerry strode back in, glanced her way, and stood in front of her. She could tell by his hard expression that something was up, and for a moment she didn't know if he was about to lecture her or not.

"Taz is right, Naomi," he said. "You screwed up this one. Walk away. You're done. But about the address, I gave it to him when your dad and I went to visit him last night. Your dad made it clear to him as well that you're no longer working there. We never shared the fact that you were undercover, doing a story on him. The moment that bar customer assaulted you, you had to know what would happen, how your dad would react. You put yourself in a situation where even those trained in that kind of area could have been hurt. I know this because I've made a business of protecting people from just this kind of thing. You weren't safe. Girls who work in a place like that have a lot more street smarts, being around that kind of thing, the behavior, knowing what they can handle. That includes knowing not to walk in darkened hallways alone."

Yeah, he was mad. She hadn't expected that. He ran his hand over the back of his head and glanced down and over to his wife. It was so sharp and rattled, and Taz seemed to be just taking it all in. "You talk some sense into her?" he said.

Taz shook her head. "It's her career, her work. I understand that. I can see someone taking on his story, but I think this one is out of reach, Naomi. Especially now, it's a moot point. You heard him. He knows who you are now, and he's right pissed, so let it go." Taz looked to Jerry with such love and something else that had Naomi wanting someone she too could share with. She was lonely without a partner, someone to love.

"Wait, he said he offered you a job?" she said. Jerry and his security business could access everything she couldn't. This was even better.

"Whatever you're thinking, the answer is no. He wanted to hire me, but I'm not getting involved in this. I can afford to pick my clients, can afford to say no. No matter what I think of the man, this whole thing, I can't take it because of you." Jerry reached for Taz, his hand to the small of her back. "You ready?"

Taz said nothing.

"What does that mean, what you think of him?" Naomi said. There was something in the way he said it that had her needing to know. That curious part of her that hated secrets, hated being the one in the dark, made her always stick her nose in things and question everything.

He glanced once to Taz and then back to Naomi. "Okay, you may not want to hear this, but I think there's more to Cameron than you know. You may not have your facts right about him."

She hadn't expected that, not from Jerry. "Are you kidding? It was just last year the article came out about him, then news reports—"

Jerry touched her shoulder. "Stop. I don't give a shit about news articles and stories that led to nothing, and that's all they were. Sure, he's been linked to some questionable things, being a commercial agent and getting money from offshore companies, hiding money. However, that's something this state's tax laws actually allow, so is it just that you're interested in the scandal, the women, in him having been accused in the press of being a dog? There are no charges against him. The thing is, Naomi, there's the truth, there's public sensationalism, and then there's printing something on speculation with no facts to back it up." Jerry was giving her a pointed look. It was intense, and she'd never before experienced this side of her brother-in-law. "If he is as bad as you believe, then there would be an investigation at play. I can honestly tell you there's nothing in any way that ties Cameron Donnelly to any of the things you or that damning article suspect him of."

"Well, if you believe that, Jerry, why don't you take the job? Prove me wrong." She threw out the challenge to him, hoping he'd take it and get in there and see firsthand how right she was. Then she'd convince him to share every piece of dirt on the man so she could write the story and show her boss and the big-time papers that Naomi Parker was cut out for those exciting jobs, those stories that only the best reporters got a shot at. "Please, Jerry, just hear me out, reconsider the job. You in there…"

"No!" He cut her off, and she'd never seen him this upset. Taz rested her hand on his chest, rubbing, appearing calmer and very much the peacemaker, taking in both of them. "You're absolutely out of your mind. Are you not hearing what I'm saying? If I took this job for Cameron, I would be working for Cameron, doing a job for Cameron, not digging up dirt or secrets or whatever else you need on him. He'd be a client, my client, and clients are protected. Their confidentiality is protected. Not even for you would I ever betray that," Jerry said with finality.

Naomi could feel this story slipping away, which would put her at a desk, doing a column that would never lead to anything—and Cameron Donnelly would be gone.

Chapter Fifteen

"She's a fucking reporter," Cameron said. "You want me to say you were right? Now's your chance. Come on, gloat and tell me you were right about her. Take a moment and rub it in. It's your moment, seriously. I mean it: Say it!" He could feel his adrenaline pumping, feeling his veins pulsing in his neck from how mad he still was.

Normally, something like this wouldn't have stuck with him for this long, but considering his luck with women, his history with being screwed over by them, he wondered whether he had a massive target on his back for women trying to fuck him over—starting with his mother, Lori. He shouldn't have been surprised by Naomi being a reporter trying to…what? Dig up something on him or create something that expanded on the story from just the year before, a story that had affected his life, turning it to shit for months. Again someone was trying to turn everything in his life upside down.

He didn't have a clue why this was happening, what her reason was for coming after him, or why women were so quick to see him as the devil. Maybe he wasn't a saint, and his personality was harsh and blunt and at times could be cutting and cruel, mainly because he had zero bullshit tolerance, hated idiots and liars more, and had a knack of making enemies faster than he did friends. Then there was Naomi and the fact that he couldn't shake an obsessive need to know everything about her. Who was she, and why was she dead set on fucking him over?

Dean lifted a longneck bottle of beer and took a drink, saying nothing, just as he'd done the moment he'd arrived at Cameron's after he'd called, yelling, freaking out, and relaying the truth of what he'd learned. Here Dean was with his socked feet up on the square glass coffee table. His jeans were faded, and his white and black T-shirt hung loosely over his large frame.

"Say something, anything," Cameron finally said. His leather shoes had left bits of dirt on the thick cream area rug, but he didn't give a shit at this point as he slid off his suit jacket and dumped it on the empty chair before unbuttoning the cuffs of his starched blue dress shirt, rolling up the sleeves to his elbows, and pushing them up further, doing everything he could to work off his rage, which only continued to build instead of fading.

"Yoga is something you should consider," Dean said.

"What?" He stared down at his brother, wondering whether he'd lost his mind.

"Yoga. It was something I learned in rehab. It calms the mind, helps center you and refocus especially in times of stress. It's more than what people think and not solely a chick thing. Grounding is important." He took another swallow, his deep brown eyes not leaving Cameron's, not adding anything else.

"I'm not doing yoga." He dropped down onto the sofa across from Dean, taking a bottle from the open case of six sitting in the middle of the coffee table and staring at it. "Alcohol free, seriously?"

Dean shrugged. "The thing with being an addict is it kind of applies to everything, alcohol too. Drinking just leads to smoking and then craving something stronger. Then I'm snorting and shooting up, a cycle I've been through how many times? I've learned the hard way that indulgence will not solve your problems. That wonderful oblivion that frees you for a moment from all the bullshit of life and stress is a temporary escape which makes coming back to the reality you were trying to forget a rude awakening. You only discover it's just as bad as you thought, or worse, and that leads to more and more snorting, smoking, or shooting up. Your life goes to shit because you haven't a fucking clue how to fix it, how to fix yourself. So yeah, alcohol free, because I intend to keep both my feet firmly planted in the present, in this fucked-up reality, and deal with everything coming at me, good or bad.

"You, though, this is about you, and you don't need me to say anything about the girl, to gloat and point out how you should've taken my advice and listened to what I was saying about the broad when I knew something was off about her the moment she stepped into that office, wobbling on those heels she could barely walk in. She was pretending something, I knew only that much, because I lived in that world. Reporter? Yeah, didn't see that one coming, but I knew it was something. Ah, don't worry about it. Just thank your lucky stars you found out now, and be grateful, because it seems, even as bad as it sounds, that scumbag drunk who tried to drag her out of there may have saved your ass."

"You seriously want me to be grateful to some piece of shit who was going to rape or kill her? Seems a bit harsh, even for you," Cameron said, putting the beer down. If he was going to have something to drink, it was going to be the real deal, something strong and preferably with a sharp bite.

"Just saying, learned a long time ago things happen for a reason, good or bad. This one now has your attention, but move on. Maybe it's time to drop this crusade of finding out who else was screwing you. I get it, I really do, but there's wisdom in knowing when to cut your losses." Dean was peeling at the label on the bottle, studying it as if it held all the answers.

Cameron shook his head, feeling the stubbornness kick in the way it did when he wasn't going to let something go. He knew he couldn't walk away because he'd already dug his heels in. "Tell me then what reason you think a mother has to screw her own son over."

"Ah, I see we're still there." Dean smiled again, glancing over and then back down at his beer.

Cameron knew his brother never gave their mother a second thought. Even as boys, Dean had never been the favorite, always getting criticized, never praised, never loved.

"Well, Lori, as I remember, was always out for number one. Just never knew why you couldn't see it. So you've got some road rash on your ass. Suck it up. At least you now know, and you're still intact, so be a big boy and move on."

How he could he say that? "It wasn't your name she used," Cameron said.

Dean was shaking his head, the bottle on his lap as he rested his hand over the back of the sofa. "No, but then, you pretty much handed her the keys to your kingdom. Even Dad was smarter than that. Maybe why he divorced her all those years ago. But you went into business with her, and she screwed you over royally, was doing things behind your back. You didn't notice the shell company she created until the shit hit the fan, and then she had you tied to being the contact person, the one skimming all the money from those import/export companies in Asia and the Middle East. Seriously, my favorite was all those scammers from Russia, Ukraine, Africa, Libya. Yeah, that was…genius, even for her." His brother let out a rather sarcastic laugh that reminded him of the horror he'd felt when he discovered the money that had come with his mother's lies and who it had tied him to.

Dean had saved him only days out of rehab, but Lori had pulled up with what he figured was fourteen million and change in dirty commission money and disappeared, leaving him with a stable of problems and companies he'd never in a million years have been associated with.

"But the strip clubs, that was genius on her part because it kind of diverted your attention from what she was really doing. I mean, she bought them, convincing you it was just another business to add to what you already owned, and a lucrative one, at that."

"I should've dumped the strip clubs or closed them up as soon as I figured it out," he said, but he'd been drowning after his life had been ripped apart, discovering what Lori did, the lies, the deception, and hit from the sidelines when that damning story had come out. His life had been in the headlines, speculation and half truths, and he did the one thing his brother had said to do, nothing at all, even though at times he'd wanted to say something, anything, to clear his name and stop the rampant talk that was fueled by hearsay, the gossip that had even his girlfriend, Kari, turning her back, believing he was a monster and walking away. That was only after she'd added her own two cents to the fire. Maybe that was why he hated women as much as he did.

"Hindsight is a bitter pill, best not taken ever," Dean said. "Ask me. I know."

His phone rang from where it rested on the large island in the kitchen. He could see it beside his wallet, his keys, the screen lit up. He didn't want to answer, but considering how things were continuing to roll for him, ignoring it may not have been the wisest course of action. He moved to it and noted the name on screen, Jerry O'Rourke. His thumb wavered over the decline button, but he accepted it. "Hello?" he said, waiting, wondering what now.

"Cameron, Jerry here. Was wondering if you'd meet with me."

Now why would he want to do that? Half a dozen reasons went through his mind in that instant. Maybe Julie or rather Naomi was hurt, or someone else was trying to screw him over. Why the hell was Jerry now calling him?

"Why would I have any interest in doing that?" Cameron asked, thinking he should hang up and block this guy from calling him again, but at the same time he needed to know what he wanted.

"Because you extended me an offer to hire my security firm."

He seriously couldn't think the offer would still be on the table. Jerry was a smart man and couldn't be so naive as to think that could be possible. "I did before I knew your sister-in-law pretended to be something she's not and lied about who she was, some reporter trying to, what, get some big scoop on me and create more lies?" He could feel his anger rising again, but then, it hadn't really faded. It was always there at the edge, just waiting to blow when something else cropped up to bite him in the ass. He could hear Jerry sigh.

"Yeah, I can't apologize for her, and we never knew she was planning this. We kind of just discovered what she was doing. But I'm not calling to talk about Naomi and how she shouldn't or should have done what she did. She's a big girl, but she's my wife's sister, family. However, my business is my business, and I think we should meet again and talk about what you're looking for, if you're still interested. If not, just tell me to fuck off, and I'll hang up and chalk this up to, I don't know, a missed opportunity."

Cameron looked over at his brother, who was relaxing on the sofa, his gaze intent, taking in everything he was saying. "Okay, say we meet, talk, then what? You sign a nondisclosure, or do you share everything with Naomi and my private business is suddenly on the front page?"

"That's not how I do business, Cameron. I think you probably took some time to check me out, my company. After doing that, I'm sure you would understand that confidentiality is the price of doing business. It is my business. If I disclose or share anything about my clients, I'll have no clients."

Fair enough, and he had seen that from making calls and Googling his company, seeing the kind of business Jerry ran. He handled everyone from senators to stars and everything in between, some of the most scandalous and talked about, and everything about Jerry and his team came up low to nonexistent on the radar. His company was established, busy, and Cameron had seen not a peep of anything scandalous about his team or his clients.

He hesitated, sensing Dean ready to tell him not to be an idiot, so he turned away, looking out the wall of windows from the kitchen and living room, through which he could see the western skyline, the reds and yellows, the beauty of the afternoon in this part of the country. He couldn't imagine living anywhere else. "Okay, Jerry. Let's meet."

Chapter Sixteen

Chris and Ivy were walking hand in hand as they stepped out of Ivy's cottage, where they both lived, arms around each other, pressed together so closely that she didn't think there was any space left between them. His cat, a black scruffy thing, hopped off the porch and darted around the side, and Ivy was laughing at something Chris said, appearing so happy and relaxed as he slipped his hand in her back jeans pocket and leaned in and kissed her nose. Totally hot, totally possessive. Anyone could see how she belonged to him. Naomi fisted her hand in her shirt at her chest, standing in the shadows, gawking like a peeping Tom. It was ridiculous, yet she was mesmerized by what seemed to be growing between them, something that said they were each other's perfect partner.

"Naomi?" she heard her sister call as she looked up and saw them both watching her.

"Sorry, I, uh…" She didn't want to talk, feeling so much like an introvert, wanting nothing more than to press her back to the wall, but she couldn't—not the way they were watching, waiting for her to say or do something. A response was needed, so she did the only thing her body would allow: She started walking over to where they stood together, Chris with no intention of letting Ivy go.

"You okay?" Chris said.

She wondered what he thought of her, and she found she had to pull her arms around herself even though she had on a sweater, a loose brown one, over her pink buttoned-up shirt. Her jeans were baggy, and she wore flip-flops on her bare feet. She was covered up, well covered.

"Yeah, I'm…good," she said even though she felt like a piece of shit after Cameron learned what she'd done. She didn't think she'd ever forget the way he stared at her as if she were the one who'd betrayed him. It wasn't that way, really, considering who he was, so why was her conscience poking at her as if telling her something else?

"You sure? What you went through, that can really mess with you. It's okay not to be." It surprised her, Chris saying that as he held tight to Ivy, who seemed very much on the same page.

The mist that burned at her eyes made her seriously pissed. What was wrong with her? She didn't cry, not over something like this. She glanced over to the house, seeing Taz waving from the porch. So they were still here. "Well, guess everyone's here for dinner," she said, fighting the urge to go back to her cabin and hide out. Someone would come knocking, or maybe her family would just as soon not look at her right now, which only added to the feeling of unwantedness she couldn't shake.

"Mom cooked a ham, and Chris I have some news we want to share," Ivy said, smiling. "Come on," she added softly with a tilt of her head as they walked the rest of the way, Naomi beside her.

She could smell the ham and everything else that went

along with it as they started up the steps, and normally that would have had her mouth watering, just not today. She was the last in the house, which was hopping. Her dad was in the living room, sitting in the easy chair, glasses on the end of his nose, reading a paperback. He put it down, pulled off his glasses, and laid them on top. Reading wasn't something he did often, and she wondered, why now? Considering the tension and how he took her in, his jaw set in the way of a man pushed further than he should have been, she realized it may have been his way of settling himself.

Mason, Scarlett, and Taz were in the kitchen with her mom, putting food out and chatting. She didn't see Jerry.

"Everyone, come on in here. We have some news to share," Ivy called out.

Naomi realized she and Chris were beaming, still glued together.

"What is it?" Her mom walked in, wiping her hands with a dishtowel and glancing over to Naomi, who was doing her best to stay in the shadows. Maybe it was the disappointment she knew her mom had to be dwelling on.

Ivy held her hand up in front of her. "Chris proposed, and I've said yes. We're getting married."

There was laughing, and Scarlett shrieked. Mason hugged Chris and then Ivy. Her dad was in there, too, shaking Chris's hand, beaming. She could see how close Chris and her father had become, considering he'd left everything for Ivy and had started over in Kaycee, building a business from scratch and working with his hands, welding, taking on anything he could pick up, at times jointly with her dad. Her mom had tears on her face, her hands on her cheeks, and she was hugging Ivy. Everyone was so happy. Then there was Ivy herself, who was happier than she'd ever seen her.

Naomi's heart was aching, unable to feel any of their joy. She heard footsteps on wood followed by the squeak of the screen door beside her. She glanced over as Jerry stepped in. He was only inches from her, taking in the scene, and then Taz bounced over to him and slid her arms around his neck, his ring glittering on her finger. Naomi had to look away, needing to slip outside and away from all of this. It was too much and made her want to weep instead of sharing in the joy of the moment.

A hand touched her arm, and she glanced over to see Jerry watching her, Taz pressed against him, his other arm around her waist. "I want to talk to you," he said. She couldn't help wondering what bomb was about to be dropped next.

Everyone was quiet, watching her, and for the first time with her family, her face heated at the unwanted attention.

"Taz and I will be sticking around for a bit," Jerry said. "I want you to know, everyone to know, that I met with Cameron Donnelly, and I'll be handling some security for him."

There was silence in the room. She could hear the wall clock ticking.

She couldn't take any more as her throat thickened, feeling as if she were the bad guy. A choice had been made, and it wasn't for her. It was a feeling of family choosing someone else against her. It was lonely and bitter, and it hurt like nothing she'd ever experienced. It was worse than being attacked. She nodded, lifted her hand to press open the screen door, and left.

Chapter Seventeen

No one followed her as she dragged herself back to her cabin and slipped inside, closing the door. She allowed herself to fall apart alone, allowing everything in that moment to hit her with full impact as she fell to pieces, sliding down to the floor. After, she was left with this feeling of being drained. She managed to wipe her nose, which ached mercilessly, and she was left with wanting—no, needing nothing more than to sleep for a day or two in silence.

As the evening started to settle in, she made her way over to the sofa and curled up on her side in her darkened living room, listening to the evening sounds, the dogs barking and then laughter from her parents' place as the screen door squeaked. She pictured Taz and Jerry, Chris and Ivy, and maybe Mason and Scarlett stepping outside. Maybe her mom and dad were there too, reveling in the happy celebration. She was could feel a building tension and something else inside her for a second, pity that made her feel even less as she lay on her side, pulling her knees up tighter to her chest.

Footsteps sounded outside, creaking on the porch step and coming closer to her door, which had her heart jack-hammering in her chest. Her hands were tucked under her cheek, which was the only part of her face that didn't hurt as she faced the door, waiting to see who it was who figured he or she had a right to intrude on her privacy. There was no knock as the door opened, and she saw her mother wearing a soft blue sweater, jeans, and old sneakers, carrying a plate covered with tinfoil. Her hair was loose, tucked behind her ears, and her eyes seemed to take in everything as she flicked on the kitchen light, set the plate down on the kitchen table, and closed the door behind her.

She knew her mom had seen her, yet she said nothing as she walked into the kitchen and pulled open a drawer to lift out a knife and fork and set them on the table. She pulled a glass from her cupboard, too, and turned on the tap to fill it with water. She set it on the table beside the plate before resting her hands on the chair back and turning her head to Naomi but not meeting her gaze. She was taking in the floor, the walls, the room, and then her hands as if needing to settle herself. Maybe that was what it was. Or maybe she didn't have a clue what to say to her middle child.

She patted the table. "I made you a plate. Come here and eat something."

Naomi didn't have the energy or the appetite, so she simply shook her head. Her mother sighed and pushed away from the table, striding toward Naomi and taking her time until she stood over her.

"I understand you needing some time and feeling as if the rug has been pulled out from under you," she said, and that made Naomi feel even worse, "but there are more sides to this than you know."

"There are no sides. Taz's husband chose business over

family, and, worse, this was my job. He's competing against me as if my job, my career, are meaningless and I don't matter. It's cruel, and you all chose to ignore it and side with him. It's simple, really. He should have chosen me, no matter what, but instead he chose the enemy, so I guess that kind of leaves the big question of where does that leave me? Up the creek and at a desk, doing a dead-end column that will earn me a minor paycheck and not much else." She pushed up to a sitting position, her feet planted firmly on the edge of the sofa now, her knees pulled up so she could wrap her arms around them. Even that didn't lessen the giant aching pit that filled her stomach.

"I guess I can see how you would think that, but you couldn't be further from the truth."

Naomi didn't like the expression on her mom's face, as if she were about to give her a scolding, as she'd done when she was a girl. "Really?" she said. "I guess you and I see things differently."

Her head ached, and the bridge of her nose felt more swollen than she'd expected, which only added to her discomfort as she pressed her hand to her temple, trying to break up some of the building tension.

"Naomi, don't be like that. I realize you're a little out of sorts, and I know that man attacking you the way he did shook you up more than you'll admit. I can see it, and as much as you were sensitive and quiet before this, you've lost your footing. I see that spooked look in your expression as if you don't know which way to step. Add in Mr. Donnelly showing up here, saying the things he did…" Her mom lifted her hand as if she understood everything about the situation. "He had a right to be upset. However, you going after a story, investigating, is also right to a point as long as you go about it the right way, looking for the facts, printing the facts, verifying your sources. There have been many hidden stories uncovered and printed, exposing some truly horrific crimes against the most vulnerable in the world."

"Cameron Donnelly is a bad man who profits—"

Her mom was shaking her head. "I think you need to talk to Jerry. As I said to you this morning, I don't think the reasons you have for going after Cameron are as simple as what you believe. I never did. If Jerry took the job with Cameron, it wasn't to hurt you. He took the job because of you," she said and then turned away, starting back to the door. "Eat your dinner, Naomi, and then go and talk to Jerry."

Chapter Eighteen

It appeared to be a bachelor party on one side, Jerry thought. The men were in their early twenties, already drunk and one getting a lap dance from one of the strippers. The rest of the bar was filled with rig workers, and the place was hopping. Waitresses dressed in as little as possible weaved their way through the pawing hands. He didn't miss the men who'd take liberties, touching a waitress's ass and then laughing and joking.

He took in the bartender, the dark-haired guy he'd seen before, and then one of his men, big, solid, and built like a tank, who was now moving through the bar and stepping over to the man with the free hand to issue a stern warning: No touching. He watched the scene. Already something had changed in the bar, going from the out-of-control degradation of women to something more manageable, if anything about a place like this could be considered remotely civilized.

"I see the difference already," Cameron said. "Your people are good."

Jerry took him in. He didn't seem to fit with a place like

this. He'd have thought the owner of a strip bar would have a lot more sleaze in his character, but Cameron was polished, somewhere between a gentleman, a ruthless businessman, and a man who believed in right and wrong. It was an odd combination, and he couldn't help liking him. "It's what we do. My guys are trained well. Considering the people who hire us, they have to see everything and anticipate a problem before it happens."

"You didn't ask, but I can see the way you look at me," Cameron said. "You have to be wondering why I own a place like this, considering all the other businesses I own and run."

Jerry didn't say anything for a minute. "Not really my place to ask, but now that you brought it up, why? I can see the other businesses, the coffee houses, dry cleaners, the strip malls. You collect rent, and even the laundromats and car washes make good investment sense, but a strip club and all the problems that come along with it?" He was shaking his head as Cameron smiled for the first time. It was toothy, like some, and he even flashed a dimple.

"Was Lori, who I told you about," he said, meaning his mother, a woman who could have given the devil a run for his money. "She and I went into business together. We were always close, and it seemed natural. I bought my first coffee house and started adding to it. She backed my first buy, and we were kind of partners. Next I know, years have passed, my businesses are vast, and she bought first the one in Rock Creek, smaller time, and then this one. Not long after, shit hit the fan, and she was gone. My girlfriend didn't take kindly to the heat, having her name tainted alongside mine, and next I know she too had added something, another story, painting me as a monster, only she lied, saying I had a cruel side that at times terrified her. It led everyone to believe I'd hurt a woman when nothing could be further from the truth. It seems I have a predilection for women who are both beautiful and shallow and believe the truth is in the eye of the beholder," he added.

Jerry wondered how Naomi would respond if she knew some of the truth Jerry had seen. "You know, Naomi is a nice girl. The way Robert and Susan raised their daughters, I think you should know she's not like that. It's one of the things that attracted me to Taz, the values the family has. Robert built those cabins beside the house to keep his daughters close, to protect them. If anything, all of those girls have been a little too sheltered," he added, and he wasn't sure what to make of the odd expression on Cameron's face.

"She's a reporter. She showed up here, lying to everyone to get a job, to get close to me, with every intention of finding some piece of damning evidence or dirt that would make a great story and once again bare me naked to the residents of this area. I'd say she's worse."

"I understand how you can think that," Jerry said, "but she's one of many who was evidently swayed by the original story. People are quick to believe the bad about others, and then there's always the thought of 'Well, he must have done something, or no one would be talking.' But trust me on this one: Naomi, although naive, believes in what she does. She's not a liar and she wouldn't have twisted facts to make herself look good."

"Why are you pushing so hard on this?" Cameron asked.

Jerry had to ask himself the same question. "I feel bad, is all. She got the shit kicked out of her by that drunk, and then the guy gets a slap on the wrist, barely. The way you found out she was a reporter, you had every right to react as you did, but it was bad timing. It's kind of like kicking a dog when it's down. You should understand that by no means am I trying to say what she was doing was okay, but the story has many sides. Things are never black and white, which makes everything so hard. I'm saying she's not Lori, and she's not your ex. That's all I'm saying."

He noticed movement, taking in Cameron's brother, who appeared through the door to the back. Dean looked around, spotting the two of them, and lifted his hand. It was a subtle gesture, one he understood. "I think your brother wants our attention," he said, and they both started across the bar.

"Got something you're both going to want to see," Dean said, leading the way back to the office, the hallway deserted.

Oscar, from Jerry's Denver office, was there, his light hair naturally wavy, thick and unruly, his dark-rimmed glasses perched on his nose, and his boyish features making him look fresh from high school rather than thirty-three. Oscar was the computer tech he brought in for those surveillance jobs that could be a little dicey.

"Your guy here found something," Dean said before leaning down on the desk and saying something to Oscar, who was typing over the keyboard of the open laptop.

"Yup," he said. "After we did a background on all your employees, six were flagged, three with felony convictions that were never disclosed, one owing child support with a bench warrant out for her—which is a first for me, as I thought it was guys who got stuck with that—and one whose Social Security belongs to someone who died twelve years ago."

He heard the strangled swearing from Dean, and Cameron said nothing, but Jerry already knew all of these details, having seen the report earlier via email. To him, this was nothing major, nothing that surprised him, considering he'd seen so many hidden secrets in everyone's past.

"You have names of all these people I'm going to need to fire?" Cameron said, picking up the files Oscar slid over the desk.

"You may want to hold off on that," Jerry said. "I'm thinking there's something more pressing. Am I right, Oscar?"

The young man's lip twitched in amusement as he slid the laptop around, showing a still shot from one of the installed cameras for this office. In the photo were two women.

Dean looked at Cameron as if gauging his reaction.

"Lori," Cameron said. "So she's back, and who's that with her?"

It appeared to be one of the waitresses. She was short, with a dark mop of hair, a lot of makeup, and mile-long legs in a barely decent tight skirt.

Dean replied, "That would be one of the waitresses, Taffy. She's been here how long?"

Cameron shrugged, shook his head. "Don't know. Pete would have hired her." He looked over to Jerry. "Pete's the one we caught selling drugs to customers. Well, Dean figured it out. What did you dig up on Taffy, her background?"

Oscar slid the computer back around and pulled up another screen. "Taffy is what she goes by, but her name is Tiffany Hodgson, originally from Oklahoma. Married at eighteen to her high school sweetheart, divorced a year later. No kids, and nothing appeared on her. She's clean."

Jerry wasn't sure what to think, and he waited on Cameron, remembering well their conversation. The man had been burned, and trust was not something that came easy. He was far from a saint, but Jerry was sure he wasn't the devil he was painted to be.

"Lori is my mother, our mother," Cameron said.

Dean made a face, shaking his head.

"She's the one I filled you in on, the one who had my name on the shell corporation, signed my name to the legal documents tying me to everything, the corporate account. She took millions, money that was funneled, and here she is, back?" Cameron stepped beside Dean to look down at the screen again. They were watching something, both quiet.

"Or she never left," Jerry said, taking in the scene on screen and the familiarity that existed between the women. "You have sound? This was recorded…?"

Dean tossed Jerry a sideways glance. "Last night after closing. Timestamp here is twelve after four a.m."

The video was rewound and the screens were pulled up, showing Taffy with her coat on, punching in the security code to turn off the alarm, coming in the back door. Lori was behind her in a tracksuit, her dark hair pulled into a ponytail, her head down until they stepped into the office. The door closed after the light switched on. The multiple camera screens showed how they passed by, one and then the other.

"No one followed you?" Lori asked, and Taffy shook her head.

"No one."

The men watched as Lori pushed the metal file cabinet over and then knelt down, taking a knife and poking it into the floorboards. She lifted a square piece and slid it away, then leaned down and lifted out a box. After opening it, she pulled out papers and cash.

Dean was already beside the file cabinet, pushing it aside, and Jerry could see the square cut in the floor. "Give me something sharp to lift this," he said.

Oscar pulled open the desk drawer and pulled out a letter opener. He handed it to Cameron, who jammed it into the floor, prying up the piece enough that Dean could grab the edge and lift it away. The opening in the floorboard could have held just about anything.

"Why did we not know this was here?" Cameron snapped, and Dean flicked a sharp glance his way. Of course they were thrown, Cameron more so. Dean just looked pissed. "Seriously?" he added as he reached in and pulled out a large square box. Inside were stacks of cash, thousands, and papers. The stocks were not in Cameron's name but in Lori Donnelly's. Also present was an agreement with a Chinese shell company to get millions of dollars out of China and into another company in Wyoming.

"Has to be millions in here," Dean said. "Good God, I'm almost scared to know where she got this, if it's stolen or marked or traceable. It's all here, and this too." He held up a thumb drive, which Jerry took and passed to Oscar.

"Open it. Find out what's there. Good or bad, we kind of need to know."

"I'm going to say this again even though you've signed the nondisclosure, Jerry: I need confidentiality. Whatever is on there…"

Jerry didn't miss the worry, the stress, and something that said he wasn't going to be fucked over again. "Cameron, you're my client. Whatever's there doesn't leave this room."

"Hey, guys, I think you're going to want to see this," Oscar said as he slid back the old banker's chair.

Jerry watched as Cameron stepped closer, looking at the screen, his face pale, but it was Dean who leaned in, read what was there, and said, "Holy shit. Uh, Jerry, you'd better take a look at this."

Chapter Nineteen

Taz, Ivy, Scarlett, and even Mason were over at the house with their mother, everyone over the moon about Ivy's upcoming wedding. A date had been set, as Chris and Ivy didn't want anything long and drawn out. For once, she thought her parents were also on the same page. The wedding would be held at the house, a simple ceremony, far different from the lavish spread for Taz and Jerry's wedding, which had transformed the ranch into something even Cinderella would have been proud of. There would be no tents, no expensive live band and waiters in black tie, no liquor and food that had cost a fortune. It would be something simple, small, just family and dinner.

Naomi couldn't get into any of it, the planning, the excitement, as she continued to watch the road in the distance, waiting for Jerry to come back. When she saw dust, she felt her excitement rising with it, but then she noticed the older pickup, the rusty model Chris drove. She stood there as he pulled into the cottage beside hers and stepped out, lifting his hand and looking around.

"Where is everyone?" he asked.

She just pointed to her parents' house. "Inside, planning your wedding."

Chris nodded, lifting out his faded jean jacket from the truck. His T-shirt was faded green, dusty, and his jeans were the older ones he wore when he worked. In his heavy work boots, he started over to where she was sitting at the edge of her top step, just waiting.

"How's the nose today?" he asked, stopping in front of her, his hand on the railing, resting one of his feet on the bottom step.

"Healing, better."

He glanced over to her parents' and back to her. "So why aren't you over there with your sisters?" he said.

The last thing she wanted to do was tell him that she couldn't dig up any happiness right now for him and Ivy. She was embarrassed to admit it to herself.

He nudged her foot, tucked into an older pair of sneakers. "Sometimes it's not all about you, you know. Even when life has kicked the shit out of you, it helps to share in someone's joy. Just being around them, it does find a way inside you even when you're doing everything you can to keep from drowning. One day at a time, Naomi, but do something instead of sitting here, wallowing and thinking of your problems. Reliving everything over and over isn't going to let you be happy, and it's not going to let you move on."

He didn't get it, and she didn't think she could explain it to him.

"Chris, I know what you're saying, but I can't right now. I'll get there, but I need a few days. If I go over there, I'll be like a dark funeral shroud that will take away Ivy's joy at planning a special day she deserves. So I hear you, but not yet," she added, not wanting to be pushed on this.

He nodded, taking her in and then looking up the road. "You want to talk about Jerry and the job he took?" he added, his teeth flashing. He was dark haired and so handsome, with a rough side that was so opposite of Ivy.

"Not really. Already have been raked over the coals by Mama that there's more to the story and it wasn't a matter of Jerry choosing his company, a job, over me. I need to talk to him, so here I sit, waiting for Jerry to come home. Taz said this morning he'd be back before four, and here it is, almost..." She could hear a car and looked up to see dust. "There he is," she said, standing up as Chris moved away from the steps.

"Hey, mind a little unwanted advice from your future brother-in-law?" he asked.

For the first time since the attack, she couldn't help the bit of a smile that touched her lips. "If I say no, you'll probably give it anyway, right?"

He did smile and glanced over to where Jerry was pulling up. "Yeah, only because you're family. I know Jerry well. We've been friends a long time. Your mom's right. Whatever reason he had for taking the job, it wasn't to hurt you or to choose his business over you. He wouldn't do that. Jerry's the opposite. He'd walk away from any job or contract that would end up hurting someone he cared about. So talk, but, Naomi, you also need to be able to listen."

Chapter Twenty

Jerry had just pulled open the fridge in his wife's cabin, but the only thing there was the beer he'd bought and a sandwich on a plate covered in plastic wrap, which looked fresh. He was sure Taz had made it in the event he returned hungry. "Nice," he said as he lifted it out along with a beer.

There was a tap on the door, and it opened. Naomi stuck her head in. The swelling around her nose had gone down, and the bruising was not as bad. Her glasses didn't appear to squeeze her face anymore. "Are you busy? Do you have a second?" she said, her blue eyes showing her vulnerability, her voice lacking in confidence.

"Sure, come on in. Where's Taz?" he asked before taking a huge bite of the ham and cheese sandwich, which was better than anything he'd ever grabbed from a deli. "Mmm, this is so good." He twisted off the cap of the beer, taking in the way Naomi hunched and was far from comfortable. He also knew what a sexual assault did to women, though each one of them was different. Even an unwanted touch had a way of messing with someone's confidence, rattling her until she questioned everything and there was nothing he could say to convince her otherwise. It was a process. He waited, knowing time was the only remedy. He took a swallow of beer, picking up his sandwich again.

"Over at Mom and Dad's, planning the wedding," she said, stopping on the other side of the table, resting her hand over the chair back.

"And you're not over there with them," he said.

She shook her head. "Chris already asked me and also tried the tough love thing, so save it," she snapped.

"Got it. So, need I ask how you're doing?" He wondered how long it would take her to start questioning him or laying into him for taking the job.

She glanced up, a glare to her glasses. Something haunted the blue of her eyes. "I was furious with you for taking the job with Cameron because I could only see you screwing me over." She lifted her hand to stop him from interrupting when he dropped the sandwich on the plate, swallowing what was in his mouth. "Let me just say this. Mama really laid into me last night, letting me know it wasn't as cut and dry as I thought with Cameron, you taking the job, that there was more and I needed to talk to you. Among other things, she said I was too focused on what I believed happened to be able to see the truth, and then Chris just moments ago added his two cents, saying you'd never choose a job over family or screw me over as I seem convinced you have. So I have to ask you, Jerry, why did you take the job with Cameron?"

He couldn't tell her, but at the same time he wished she knew the truth. He gestured to the chair back she was holding. "Sit down," he said as he pulled out the other pine chair across from her at the small round table and sat, pushing the plate aside but keeping his beer in front of him. "They're right, both your mom and Chris. I didn't take the job to be selfish and screw you over; I took it because of you and the fact that you were going after something that was going to end badly for you and Cameron. You were running with nothing that was factual."

"How can you say that—"

"Let me finish." He reached out and rested his hand over her slender wrist, giving it a squeeze. Feeling her tense, he pulled away. "Cameron Donnelly was crucified in the press a year ago, and you were taking all that fabrication, a lot of hearsay and speculation, the gossip, and running with it. You were posing as a two-dollar whore, waiting tables in a sleazy strip club, to get close to the man and, what?"

Her face heated with a blush that started in her cheeks. Her hands rose to cover her embarrassment as he waited for what she'd say. Maybe he'd gone too far.

"Getting close to him would get me access. I was going to go through files, get him talking, and see what leads came from that. Then I was going to work each one of them, but no chance of that now. But you're there, you see the kind of man he is. You have access to his records, what he's done, what he's doing. You could point me in a direction to start." She sounded hopeful, not getting that she was still going the wrong way.

He couldn't believe she was still focused on the story as he stood up and moved away from the table, feeling some of the simmering anger Cameron had toward her. "You don't get it. There is no story. It was all bullshit. He's not the monster you believe him to be..." He lifted his hands before he said anything else, taking in the surprise in her expression.

"How would you know this?" she asked, leaning toward him, her hands pressed to the table top.

He just shook his head. "I'm sorry, Naomi. I won't share that with you. He's my client, and even if he weren't, I still wouldn't. Word of advice, you know what sets the exceptional reporter apart from every other reporter out there?" he said, then took in her wide eyes and the way she shook her head.

"No."

"Questioning the validity of information. An exceptional reporter doesn't just print or write a story to have her name in lights. She goes after the truth and digs to get it right. She's able to keep an open mind and understand that everything is not always as it seems, that people have agendas at times and reasons for wanting to destroy someone."

She said nothing for a moment before she glanced up to him, and this time something was different. "So if what I think you're saying is correct, Cameron Donnelly didn't do the things he was said to have done. Is that what you're saying?"

He lifted the beer, took a drink, and said nothing.

"I see. So tell me this: Why did the papers and evening news run stories saying he had?"

"Great question, Naomi. Maybe that's where you should start, along with asking yourself if it wasn't the person who wrote those stories who had something to gain by destroying Cameron. Who did?"

Jerry noted how pale her face went. For the first time since arriving here days ago with Taz and seeing Naomi all painted up with an agenda, a story, and an idea that had only gotten her neck deep in trouble, Jerry saw something that had her really thinking.

Then she stood up, her hands flat on the table. When

she glanced over to Jerry again, her expression was engaged, excited, then resigned. She said, "Okay, I think I get it, but can you do me just one favor?"

He wasn't sure he was going to like this. "Maybe. It depends, Naomi," he said, and she nodded.

"Can you get me in to see Cameron?"

Chapter Twenty-One

He was holding a mug of coffee, and it was still early. Jerry had texted him and asked to meet, followed by a phone call. Cameron had heard his hesitation, followed by a direct statement: "Naomi wants to speak with you. I want to bring her, and no, I didn't share anything, but I'm asking you not to dismiss this. As I said to her, everything isn't always so black and white."

He still wasn't sure why he'd listened, why he'd agreed to such a thing, when the woman had lied and would have added to his misery. He stood outside his front door, leaning against a support beam, watching as Jerry parked his Mercedes. He took in the woman who stepped out of the passenger side—not a blonde but a woman with dark hair, glasses, and her nose still bruised. He had to wonder, why the change? She had gone from being over the top and attractive to more of who she should have been. Her hair hung straight past her butt, a very nice shade of brown. She was also in sneakers, non-designer jeans, and a navy T-shirt with a rounded neck that showed no cleavage.

She stepped over to him as Jerry came around the front. "Hey, Cameron. Thanks for this."

Jerry reached out to shake his hand, still stuck on the woman who'd tried to pretend to be someone she wasn't. He noticed then what else seemed different. Her face wasn't caked with heavy makeup, and she looked nice. It was refreshing and wholesome, and there was something about the look that he liked. He said nothing to her as he crossed his arms, keeping his hands close to him as she shot Jerry a panicked glance.

"This is your deal, Naomi," Jerry said. "Cameron has agreed to meet you." Then he walked back to the driver's door and pulled it open.

"Where are you going?" Cameron asked as Naomi paled.

"I'm going to meet Dean at the club, and Oscar, and that lawyer you hired. You can stay here and talk with Naomi. But a word of advice, Cameron: She's my sister-in-law, so have some respect, please. And, Naomi…" He said nothing else, but Cameron didn't miss the warning. Naomi nodded as Jerry climbed behind the wheel and then pulled away.

"Thanks for meeting me," she said, looking up at him with big blue eyes behind glasses that were plain and simple, with a dark rim.

"Sure. Can I get you something, tea, water, coffee?" he said, still holding his mug, which was now empty.

She shook her head. "No, had enough already, and it'll only add to my nerves." She was squeezing the strap of the purse slung over her shoulder, far from relaxed.

"I'm dying of curiosity," he said as he started to the door. "Why this meeting?"

She followed, and he took in her flush, the pink in her cheeks, as she took in his place. Yes, it was huge and impressive and well furnished and all his. "Because of so many things. Because I may have gotten something wrong, being convinced that things happened only one way, that the media had already tried you and you were therefor guilty. I saw only that and didn't consider for one second that there could be any possibility of something different."

He gestured to the stool at the kitchen island. She pulled it out and sat, resting her purse on the counter, and for a moment he wanted to ask her to open it and see whether there was a recorder or whether her cell phone was set to record. Maybe she knew by the way he stared, as she unzipped the bag and held it over to him.

"I guess I deserve that. Go ahead, but there's nothing in there but a wallet, a brush, a few unmentionables, and likely six dollars and change. My cell phone is here, and it's turned off." She held it up.

He waved off the bag, and she moved it beside her. "Okay, so is this an apology?" he said. He didn't have a clue why she was here. What could she possibly want?

She shook her head and then shrugged. "Yes and no. I want to do a story on you that tells the truth, that…"

"No fucking way. No!" he shouted and lifted his hands in the air. He couldn't believe he was back here again with just another angle.

She was off her stool and over in front of him. Her hand touched his arm. "Cameron, please hear me out. Please," she said, and her expression and her eyes staring up at him were the only reason he agreed.

"Fine, but no bullshit, Naomi. I'm so tired of the deception."

She stood where she was, nodding, pressing her hands together. "I get it, Cameron. I do. As I thought about it, the story and everything that was said about you, I realized there were no charges or fines or any action of any kind taken against you. I never thought about it before except to think that you just got away with it. Then I realized, everything coming back on you, it seemed so easy, and you never said one word to defend yourself, but after some digging, I found that Lori Donnelly was the one at the corporate head, buying, making deals, and you were only running your small business, the coffee house you managed, the car washes, cleaners, laundromats. She was the one arranging the deals, and you were focused on the day to day. She was your mother, and she was the one responsible, not you. But then there was another woman…" She reached for her purse, pulled out a small notepad, and flipped it open. He could tell she was searching for a name as she read her scribbles. "A Kari, who was interviewed and said you were…" She stopped, looking down again, frowning.

"She said I was a twisted fuck with a mean streak who would screw over his own mother in a second, and that every allegation would be absolutely true. Or something along those lines," he added, remembering when the reporters had started calling, the heat that had come at him. He'd discovered who his friends were and weren't, and Kari definitely wasn't one of them. She'd bolted and tossed him to the wolves to save her own skin and make sure the scandal didn't touch her at all.

"Yeah, that. Do you know why she said it?" There it was, that curiosity, the questioning that he'd never agreed to.

"No, I don't, but then, I stopped trying to figure out why a woman would screw over a man. Seems I attract those who practice the art of deception, apparently beginning at an early age."

She appeared confused by the odd look on her face.

"My mother, Lori," he said.

Her mouth made a big O, and for a moment she was quiet. "So your girlfriend…"

"Ex, and good riddance."

"Okay, your ex-girlfriend, she just said those things about you and you have no idea why?"

He wondered if she understood what she was asking. "You mean why would anyone lash out to hurt someone she's supposedly in love with? Why would anyone randomly listen to gossip and believe the word of a stranger? It's because it's so juicy that everyone jumps into it, twisting it, and then all of a sudden friends you never thought you had appear and are interviewed and you're wondering, 'Who the fuck is that?' All they were doing was looking for their own fifteen minutes of fame, yet every one of those people had nothing factual to back anything up. Nothing was vetted. The stories read almost like bestselling pieces of fiction, but it was my life on those front pages, in the news, being ripped apart, all because my mother was doing something she shouldn't have, and I was the one who was completely blind to her."

Except that his mother's hand was now caught in the proverbial cookie jar. The evidence was there. It was what they'd found on the flash drive, which went back to the beginning and the first day he'd bought his first business, the coffee house. It was one damning email that would seal Lori's fate, one where she was advised to sign Cameron's name and keep hers off all official documents. He said nothing to Naomi. Jerry knew, his brother knew, and now his lawyers did, too, but no one else ever would.

"Any more questions?" he asked and took in how pale her face was.

"No. I'm sorry about your mother. I can't imagine." She shrugged. "And your girlfriend, that is…not right," she said, her brows quirking. Something about the way she moved eased his irritation with her.

"It is what it is, Naomi. Let it go—and no story," he added, moving over to his espresso machine. He added coffee grounds and water, slipped his cup under, and turned it on, taking in the horror on her face as if he'd said the most ridiculous thing ever.

"You can't be serious. You need to have your story told, the truth out there of what really happened and that it wasn't you. People need to know the truth." She sounded really mad, and her hand fisted on his counter. He turned off his espresso maker and took in the fight and passion and something else there that softened his heart to her.

"No, actually, they don't, and I'll tell you why. You could print a new story telling the truth of what really happened, and people would say, 'Him in the news again, another scandal?' Maybe some people would believe it, but there would be those who'd say I have to be guilty of something. I have to have done something. No, there really are times that it's best to let things die a slow death. People will forget, move on, and there will be something else, but there will not be another story about me," he said, stepping closer to her, taking in the passion still on her face as if she couldn't believe he could just be okay with this.

"Cameron, it's not right," she said, her hand on her hip.

"No, it's not, but it happens, and I for one am not wasting one more minute thinking about it. So how are you doing?" He watched as she touched her face. "And your hair." He gestured to it, and she lifted her hand over the back of her head.

"It's my natural color. The blond was too much of a reminder of what almost happened. I'm fine, though. I will be."

What was it about her now that he was seeing her differently?

"So a reporter, really?" he said. "Seriously, I never saw that one coming."

She smiled, and it really was lovely. "You sure I can't convince you to sit down with me, tell your story?"

He shook his head. "Nope. Let it go, Naomi," he said, but instead of stubbornness, he saw something he'd never seen on the face of a woman before: such honest emotion. He couldn't help himself as he took her in, the picture of something different, something real. He realized then the possibility of something that could happen here. "Naomi, will you have dinner with me?" he said.

To his surprise, she nodded and said, "Cameron, I would love to have dinner with you."

Chapter Twenty-Two

"You can't be serious!" Taz said. Her dark wavy hair was pinned up in a messy bun, and she was wearing one of Naomi's casual sundresses, a loose blue and white cotton one with pockets that stopped above the knees, sleeveless and buttoned up. She and Jerry hadn't packed for an extended stay, and she was tired of doing laundry. She leaned against the bathroom door, watching Naomi put the finishing touches on her makeup, covering up the blue and green bruising around her nose and applying light shadow and mascara. The image staring back was of the Naomi she was used to.

"I am not quite sure where the problem is. What's the big deal?" Naomi said. Of course she was quite aware of how it looked. Cameron showing up at the house to take her for dinner had everyone wondering whether she'd lost her mind.

"For one, it was just this week you met the man and were hell bent on doing an investigative story on his scandals, just in case you've forgotten. Now here you are going to dinner with him when only days, hours ago you were ready to nail his ass to the wall and destroy him. You called him a monster, among other things, and now after one meeting and a conversation, he asks you for dinner and that's it, all's forgiven, and you're going?" Taz crossed her arms. She appeared a little pale, frowning. She pressed her hand to her forehead and swallowed.

"I was wrong about him," Naomi said. He really is quite handsome, and there's something about him that has me wanting to get to know him a little better." The attraction that had zinged when she was around him had only added to her anger before. She'd thought he was a destroyer of women, when really it was the other way around. Now she couldn't shake the sense she was seeing him with her eyes wide open. She looked back at Taz. "Are you okay? You look pale and a little off."

Taz said nothing, and she glanced back at herself in the mirror. With enough cover-up on her face, she looked almost normal. Even the swelling of her nose had gone down, returning it to its normal perky shape. "I thought you'd be a little more supportive, considering your husband is working for him and was the one to point out to me how wrong I was about him. Knowing now what happened, I feel guilty for jumping onto the bandwagon of judging and damning him based purely on someone's accusation, someone with an ax to grind, which there was no basis for. You know what it reminded me of, and it just hit me, is the Salem witch trials. The basis was the same, an accusation and hysteria that followed, only now the trial takes place in the paper or on TV." At least society had evolved enough that they weren't stringing him up—yet. She really did need to clear his name.

She looked over to Taz again, expecting her to add her two or three cents, as she ran a brush through her long hair, holding the length to get the tangles out at the ends.

Her sister had her hand pressed to her forehead, her other on her stomach. "You okay? You don't look so good."

Taz dropped her hand and moved away from the door, blowing out a breath. "I'm late," she said, looking away.

"What are you late for? I didn't realize you were planning to go anywhere..." It hit her when Taz leveled her with a hard look as if to say, *You idiot.* "Oh, you mean, like a baby?" she said, taking in what it meant, another grandchild for her parents and Taz becoming a mother.

"Yes, that late." She stepped away from the doorway, and Naomi followed her.

"Does Jerry know? How far along are you?" she asked, a million things running through her mind along with the fact that Cameron would be there any minute.

"I don't know for sure yet, just a feeling. I haven't taken a pregnancy test. Was going to tell him, but he's preoccupied with this job for Cameron. Don't say anything, because I didn't mean to tell anyone, not yet. Jerry should be the first to know."

Naomi heard a car, and Taz was at the door, opening it.

"Cameron is here," Taz said, stepping onto the front porch. "I mean it, Naomi. Keep what I said to yourself. And about Cameron, please think about what I said. Even though he may not have done what he was accused of, there's still the shadow of a guilty man around him, and it will follow him. You need to be prepared for that, because there will always be those who'll say he must have done something even though he didn't. It's just human nature. Flawed, yes, but human nature."

Then she left. Naomi heard her saying something to Cameron, and he appeared in the doorway, fit, tall, in blue jeans, a white dress shirt, and shades. He was serious man candy, the way he filled the doorway, and it wasn't lost on her that there was nothing about him that was the least bit cocky.

~

"JERRY TOLD me your dad built these cottages," Cameron said.

Naomi appeared a little rattled but gorgeous in a simple sleeveless black and white dress that stopped just above her knees and had a high rounded neckline. Her dark hair hung straight past her butt, long and loose.

"Yeah, kind of a long story. Dad and Mom were worried after what happened with my oldest sister, Brandyne. He wanted to keep his daughters close," she said. It wasn't lost on him how nervous she seemed, not the confident woman who'd begged him for a job in the strip club. She looked down, pushing up her glasses, which had slipped down her nose, and pulling her lip between her teeth.

"You look nice," he said. Sexy, really. Even her heels weren't overly high, just simple sandals, her toenails painted pink.

She blushed. "Thank you. Wasn't sure what to wear, as you didn't say where we were going for dinner."

"You look fine, great. Thought we'd try this barbecue place just outside Buffalo. It's a drive, but it's supposed to be worth it."

She paled. "Sounds really casual. Maybe I should change?" She took a step, gesturing to a set of stairs that went up to a loft, where he could see a bed. It was a small cabin, maybe five hundred square feet, tops.

He shook his head. "No need. You look perfect," he said, holding out his hand. She hesitated only a second before slipping hers into it, soft, slender, warm, and he guided her out.

There was Robert Parker, a man he'd never forget, standing at the bottom of the steps, his arms crossed. Jerry was behind him, looking awkward and uncomfortable. They were now meeting in a different time, a different place, and under different circumstances entirely—but what hadn't changed was that they still cared about Naomi.

Chapter Twenty-Three

"Daddy, uh…" She came up short, feeling the heat from Cameron behind her as she stared down at her father, who was standing there now with an expression that was anything but friendly.

"So what is this?" Robert gestured between them, and she took in Jerry, who was shaking his head behind her dad. Was it a warning? She didn't have a clue, considering she hadn't really shared with anyone other than Taz that she was going on a date with Cameron, and Taz had already given her an earful.

"Well, Cameron and I are going out for dinner," she said, but her father was looking past her at Cameron as if she wasn't even there and this conversation didn't include her.

"I see," he said. He did glance at her then, and it was hard, no smiling. There was nothing there that said, *Have a great time.*

"I asked Naomi out for dinner, and she said yes," Cameron said. "I hope that's not a problem." He stepped around her, speaking down to her dad but staying close.

"I guess I'm a little confused, considering my daughter was writing a story about you that would have caused you considerable problems. Now, what, all is forgiven? Let's move on and forget about it? But let's not forget that you own a strip club. You're not exactly in the category of reputable men I want dating any one of my daughters."

Jerry's face was grim behind her dad, his arms crossed stiffly in front of him as if he'd had an earful already about this, or maybe there was more.

Naomi was embarrassed even after everything. "Daddy, that's not fair. It's more than that…"

Robert held up his hand to stop her. "Naomi, it is exactly that, and let me point out to you as well that it was just how many days ago that you were attacked in this man's place and put in danger, which goes to you not really making the best of choices." He sounded really mad, and this was not something she'd heard before, not something she really expected.

"You know what? This is going nowhere," Jerry said. "Robert, I seriously respect and understand your reservations about Cameron taking Naomi out for dinner and why you would feel that way, considering all that's happened, but he's not the bad guy here. He's—"

"Stop, Jerry," Cameron said.

Naomi took in her mom and Mason on the porch, watching the scene. Taz was standing a little ways away, wide eyed, as if she couldn't believe it, just as Chris and Ivy drove in from wherever they'd been in his pickup. It was a spectacle, and the only one missing was Scarlett, who lived for drama.

"No, both of you, all of you, stop," Naomi said. She set her hand on Cameron's arm, and his eyes went to her touch. She didn't know whether it was welcome or not. Her dad too didn't seem happy that she was even close to him. "Dad, I'm a grown woman, and yes, I've made some mistakes, but they're mine to make. I misjudged Cameron. I made a mistake, which isn't something I can afford to do if I want to be a good reporter. But this isn't business anymore, this is personal, and Cameron was also the one who saved me. If it wasn't for Cameron..." She had to stop, as a sick feeling hit her as she imagined the sweaty, stinking drunk again. "He got me out of there. He never wanted to hire me, and it's all on me because I was playing a role, pretending to be someone I'm not for a story all because I'm trying to make a name for myself, and I got in over my head. I wouldn't listen to anyone. Dad, even Mom isn't convinced that Cameron is a bad guy and that he did what he was accused of."

Her father glanced over to the house and lifted his chin, a gesture that had her mom and Mason popping back inside. "It's not about that," he said. "It's about the mess he was involved in. Whether he did it or not is irrelevant. There are so many other things at play, like character. You own a business that degrades women, so how do you think I'm going to react with you wanting to take my daughter out?"

Naomi didn't know what to say. The way he put it made sense and hurt at the same time. She felt hands on her shoulders. Cameron was there, and she had to look up.

"I agree with you, Mr. Parker, and if it were my daughter I'd feel the same, but there's a lot about my business that you don't know. I would like to take your daughter out for dinner. I'm not about to disrespect her and take her someplace where she would be in danger."

Naomi found herself holding her breath, reaching up and touching Cameron's hand on her shoulder as her dad glanced back to Jerry, who was rubbing his chin.

"You okay with this? You're working with him. You know more than I do?" Robert said.

Naomi stared at Jerry, waiting for what he'd say. She could feel Cameron tense behind her.

"Yeah, he's a good guy," Jerry said.

Her dad glanced back once more, taking in her and then Cameron. He didn't say anything as he nodded before starting back to the house.

Jerry's expression was priceless as he took them both in. "If I were you, I'd have her back early," he said to Cameron before letting out a soft chuckle, shaking his head, and glancing over to Taz.

Naomi looked up at Cameron, who had an odd look on his face as he watched her dad walking away. When he looked down at her with his green eyes, his expression softened and a smile touched his lips. "Well, I can honestly say I've never had a father rake me over the coals before."

Chapter Twenty-Four

Cameron watched as Naomi finished eating a plate of the best ribs he'd ever tasted. There was sauce at the edge of her lips, and she'd eaten almost her entire plate along with the cornbread and slaw that had come with the three rib bones—a woman with an appetite. She wiped her hands with a paper napkin from the stack on the picnic table at this outdoor restaurant, which was packed. He had a beer in front of him and one for Naomi. This was the kind of place he'd never have been able to take any of the women he'd dated before, including Kari, who'd have never dared to set foot there.

He gestured to her lips. "You've got a little right there."

She grabbed another napkin, a blush hitting her cheeks as she wiped and then covered her mouth, as she also had some stuck in her teeth. "That was so good. Never been here. Sorry, messy." She lifted her hands and smiled before taking a swallow of beer. It wasn't often he met a woman, or rather dated one, who liked beer. It was usually more along the lines of those fancy drinks, champagne or wine.

Then there were the girls at the strip club, the waitresses and dancers, but he hadn't really paid much attention to them, as they weren't the type of ladies he wanted to date.

"I'm sorry about my dad." Naomi leaned forward, hunching a bit, and it wasn't lost on him that the simple dress she was wearing didn't show even a hint of cleavage. What a contrast to the girls he'd met, so different.

"You've apologized half a dozen times, Naomi. It's not as bad as you're making it out to be."

Her expression was priceless, her eyes wide behind her plain glasses. He knew she had to be thinking otherwise.

"Yes, it was unexpected," he said, "but it really gave me an insight into your family and some of the mystery surrounding you. A lot of questions were answered for me tonight." He could tell she was thrown by that too.

"Like what?"

"You're quite the actress, I suppose, whether you know that or not—pretending to be someone you weren't. I sensed something wasn't right and didn't entirely work, and I would have canned you, too, because you weren't a fit for my place. Now I know why, at least, why I had that feeling about you. This is better." He wondered whether she had any idea what a turnoff it had been, the way she'd pretended to be. This was better, left more to the imagination, even though he'd had a firsthand look at her charms, considering the outfit she'd worn at the bar had done little to hide any of her fabulous figure. He gestured to her and knew by her expression she didn't get it. "This is the real you?"

She nodded. "Yes, this is me, plain, ordinary, glasses." She gestured toward them, smiling awkwardly and showing some struggling self-confidence.

"Much better," he said. She was real, the kind of

woman he felt comfortable with. His guard, which he kept up, waiting for something to come out of left field and sucker punch him, was also easing back.

"Really? I would've thought guys like you preferred the fashion model type, the lookers, the…" She was thinking, and he wondered whether she had any idea how wrong she was.

"Like one of the painted-up waitresses at the club," he said, leaning in as she nodded slowly.

"Yeah, like one of them."

That she would jump to that conclusion actually bothered him. "Don't confuse the girls who work in a place like that with fashion models," he said. Kari was the fashion type, with Gucci everything and a trainer at the gym, barely eating anything so as not to put a pound on. She'd had a shallowness he'd never really paid attention to, but he'd once seen her attitude as fun, exciting. "They're a different sort, just as you are." He lifted his beer, looking around, and swallowed the rest. "We should go," he said, taking in the panic on her face.

"Did I say something wrong?"

He stood up and waited for her to step out, taking in her long legs, the reasonable heels, and the simple dress, which didn't look like it had cost a fortune.

"I'm not like that, Naomi. Maybe a lot of people have misread me about a lot of things for a long time, but those women at the bar are exactly the kind of women I will never date. I want real," he said as she stood in front of him. "You feel like going for a drive?"

Surprise or something settled in her expression, followed by a nice easy smile, not that flashing one she'd given him at the bar. Everything he'd seen before was a role, an act, and nothing real, he realized now.

"Okay," she said, and he settled his hand on the small of her back as he walked her out of the restaurant and over to his car.

~

NAOMI LEANED against the hood of Cameron's car, taking in the valley below. It wasn't far from where she lived, and she'd never been up this way before. It was a backroad, a private pullout, and if her father knew where she was, he'd have lost it. *I'm twenty-four, not sixteen,* she had to keep reminding herself. She also couldn't believe she was thinking of her dad when she was in a piece of paradise as the sun was setting with a man she'd never have believed would give her the time of day. There was a lot to Cameron Donnelly, and he was a very complex person.

"Gorgeous, isn't it?" he said. "I discovered this a while ago, and when I came out to your place that first time, I remembered how close you lived to this. Putting it all together, there's a lot of Wyoming I've yet to see. So tell me everything about you, Naomi, the real you."

He was so close to her, leaning against the car. She could feel the heat from him. She wished he'd touch her again as she brushed close to him, wondering as she looked up to him through her glasses whether he was toying with her or really did like her. "Well, there isn't much to me. This is it, really."

The way he was watching her, she wished he'd lean in and kiss her. There was so much to him that it both terri-fied and excited her. "Oh, I think there is," he said. "You live in a cabin on your parents' property with a protective family, one with a lot of closeness, respect. Watching your response to your father even though you're an adult said a lot about you." He didn't smile. Was it too much for him? She couldn't help wondering, as he gave away nothing of what he was thinking.

"My older sister left town with a cowboy she met at the rodeo after she got pregnant, believing my parents would turn her out or something, which couldn't have been further from the truth. They had a fight and heated words, and I can still remember their faces when it was all said and done. For years they never knew where she was. None of us did. Then there was the overreaction of Daddy banning the rest of us from ever going to the rodeo, not that it did any good. We'd sneak out and never let on, but we saw what it did to my parents, the years of worry. That was why Daddy built the cabins for Taz, Ivy, and me. Scarlett is just finishing high school, and Mason has a few years, so they'll have to wait, but I'm sure their turn will come."

Now he was smiling, or was he laughing at her? She wasn't sure by the smile on his face and the way his eyes danced with light. "You respect your parents," he said, his hands curled up around the hood of the car. "That says a lot about you and your relationship with the world."

"Are you making fun of me?" She wasn't sure whether he was toying with her and wished he'd just say it.

This time, as he looked down at her, she saw it clearly in his face, the heat that flickered in his eyes. "No," he said as his fingers touched her chin, and she stared up at him, willing him closer. She wondered by the hesitation whether he was waiting for permission, yes or no, so she lifted her lips, her head moving closer, her hand touching his hard, muscled forearm, feeling the bunch and pull and his strength as his hand slid over her cheek.

He leaned in closer, his soft warm lips brushing over

hers, kissing her, tasting her, holding her face now between his hands and kissing her deeper in a way that was so possessive, taking all of her. She'd never been taken like this, kissed like this by a man before.

Chapter Twenty-Five

It had been days since her father had spoken to her, and it wasn't lost on her how upset he was. What made it worse was that he didn't know the real Cameron Donnelly. She doubted all the people who'd become his judge and jury in the press and those in the public did, either. He was a complex man who kept to himself, keeping his private life just that: private. Added to that, she didn't understand how a man could care so little of what people thought of him. Working on that would be her next goal, considering that tonight she planned to cook him dinner at his place.

She heard a car door and a trunk close, then voices, and she stepped out of her cabin to see Jerry loading up his car. Taz was sitting on the porch, and her father and Chris were putting tools in the back of his pickup. She lifted her hand to Ivy, who was carrying a go mug, dressed in her nursing scrubs, with her car door open, ready to go.

She started over as Chris slid up to Ivy, his hands around her face, kissing her deeply, closely, intimately. Naomi almost sidestepped to go around them, but then he pulled away, still holding her sister. It was something private and personal between them. He smiled deeply before glancing to her.

"Good morning, Naomi," Chris said, his expression that of a man so in love. Ivy glanced her way after Chris kissed her one more time and then walked off, lifting his hand. "We'll talk about it tonight," he said to Ivy. Naomi couldn't help wondering what that was about.

"You off to work?" she asked her sister, who set her mug on the roof of her compact.

"Yes, working a double today," she said, glancing Chris's way. He was speaking with her dad, and it wasn't lost on Naomi the way her dad glanced over.

"Everything okay?" She gestured over to Chris.

Ivy smiled. "Couldn't be better, except my soon-to-be husband isn't liking how much I'm working and wants me to cut back a bit. We set a date too, the end of the month. You weren't here last night when we told everyone. Dating Cameron again?" Ivy didn't smile. She didn't give anything in her expression to let Naomi in on what she was thinking.

"I was. I'm seeing him tonight, too. His place this time," she added, glancing over at Jerry and Taz, hand in hand.

"Do I need to be worried?" Ivy said. Chris's ring caught the morning sun on her hand, and Naomi couldn't help feeling some resentment.

"Honestly, Ivy, you haven't given Cameron a chance at all. You don't know him, yet here you are, ready to condemn him and treat me as if I don't know any better. I have feelings for the man, and just to be clear, this is my life. My choices that I get to make, not you," she added, feeling the fury and realizing she needed to go back to her cabin and get ready for work, resigned to her fate of a boring endless column that she was looking forward to writing as much as she would a root canal.

"Hey, just wait a second. That's not what I mean at all. You're right, I don't know Cameron, but I know you, and I also know this thing with him has moved really fast. Have you forgotten already that not even a week ago, you were attacked and a man tried to rape you? I'm pretty sure you haven't even given yourself time to process that," Ivy snapped, and it was so much like a slap in the face, loud enough that everyone was watching.

Once again, Naomi felt naked and humiliated. "Thank you for that, Ivy. Maybe you'd like to say it a little louder so everyone in the next county can also know my business." She stepped back, seeing the moment her sister regretted what she'd said.

"Sorry. You're right. I'm just concerned about you, is all."

She lifted her hand. "Concern yourself with you, not me—and congratulations to you and Chris. I'm happy for you," she added as an afterthought.

The tension of a lingering disagreement wasn't something unfamiliar to her, considering the number of times over the years she'd fought and disagreed with her sisters, but right now it felt different. Or maybe it was just her.

"Point taken, and thank you. Would be nice if you'd be part of the planning, Naomi," Ivy said. "Tonight, tomorrow, maybe we could talk."

She glanced over her shoulder to Taz and Jerry walking over, her dad and Chris already pulling away. "Sunday dinner?" Naomi said. "As I said, I have plans tonight." Tomorrow being Saturday, she wouldn't have to work—that was, if she had her way. Sunday was the family dinner she'd missed only a few times, one she was sure would be awkward.

Her sister nodded and then slipped into her car. "Okay, Sunday it is," she said.

As Taz and Jerry approached, Naomi stood in the wake of dust as Ivy pulled away. "You two leaving?" she asked, taking in Taz and something in her expression.

"We are. We'll be back, though. Naomi knows," she said to Jerry, who took in all of her. Everything in that one look said how much of his world revolved around her sister. It was the kind of everything she wanted.

"No one knows yet, Naomi," Taz said. "Keep it to yourself until…" She glanced to Jerry. Whatever she was thinking was only between them.

"I'm getting Taz to the doctor, mine, in Denver," he said, sliding his arm around Taz as she slid closer to him.

"So is it for sure? Are you pregnant?" She kept her voice low and took in the joy in their expressions.

"Home pregnancy test was positive, but Jerry is insisting I get checked out now by his doctor even though the one I've used all my life is here."

Jerry was shaking his head. "I want the best for you, and we live in Denver. We'll start this right, nothing second rate for my wife or child—and you need to give notice," he added. Naomi noted Taz's frown. Her sister was a paramedic, and she could see her career coming to an end, for right now, anyway.

"We'll talk about that after we know for sure," she said.

Jerry had that stubborn look on his face and was shaking his head. "I told you already, you're quitting. You don't need to work, and I want you taking it easy, not in stressful situations, lifting a heavy stretcher. No, this isn't even negotiable, Taz…"

Then they were walking away, Jerry adamant and demanding. She wondered if Taz would be able to work him down, being stubborn and headstrong. As if she realized Naomi was still there, Taz lifted her hand and waved back.

Naomi was about to head back to her cabin when she noticed her mother on the front porch, watching her. Although she'd love nothing more than to slip away, her conscience had her putting one foot in front of the other over to her mother. Susan Parker was now leaning on the rail, her shoulder-length hair pulled up, wearing a blue sleeveless shirt over a jean skirt, flip flops on her feet, taking in Jerry and Taz as they drove away and then dropping her gaze to Naomi as she stopped at the bottom of the steps.

"Was starting to think you were avoiding all of us," Susan said. "You come in and then leave again. Seeing that Cameron Donnelly an awful lot."

She sighed because she realized no one in her family was going to welcome him easily. It seemed as if everything and everyone was stacked against them, and it had so much to do with how she'd originally judged him.

"You know, Mama, you were right about him, and I… yes, I've seen him every night." Spending time with him, touching, kissing, dinner, lunch, and just spending time together. She had plans for tonight and didn't want her family waiting up for her, wondering where she was.

"So is this because of what I said? Because it seems kind of flighty even for you, Naomi. I said I don't hold much account for the news, which at times is worse than a local busybody stirring up gossip and trouble. I didn't say to start dating a man who owns a strip club and has likely associated with a lot of shady characters you shouldn't be involved with. Your father's upset too, Naomi," she added, and of course that had its desired effect.

"Well, I'm sorry to disappoint you, but for the first time in my life, I'm happy. I really like Cameron, and he makes me feel wanted, beautiful, appreciated. Whatever level of shady you think he's involved in, I've seen only the opposite. He's a gentleman and has treated me as such, and he has nothing but kind things to say about Dad. I guess I don't understand your objections, you and Daddy. After all, you welcomed both Chris and Jerry. I'm not sure I'm getting this."

"Hold on a second, Naomi. It's more about how this evolved from deception, yours to him. Now you've changed your entire opinion overnight and are dating him. That's where our problem is. I wonder if you've even considered how this entire thing could blow up in your face from the very rocky foundation it has been built on." Her mother was now standing with her hands on the rail. Mason, her younger sister, with odd ivory-colored hair now, stepped out onto the porch and took in both Susan and Naomi. She said nothing as her mother turned a tense glance her way.

"You ready for school?" Susan said. "The bus will be here soon."

"I'm ready, but I could hear you both out here, and before that I could hear Ivy, too, the way you all keep laying into Naomi."

She was surprised by her sister speaking as she did to her mom. Even her mom seemed to stand up and take notice, turning to Mason as if ready to scold her. "Excuse me?"

"Hey, I've heard you and Daddy discussing for how many nights and talking down about Naomi and her choices, but they're hers. I've not met Cameron, but I wonder if you have any idea the impression you're giving when you talk about him, considering you've always been first to point out that we should not judge others and make our own minds up about people, not allow others to form opinions for us. Seems to me that's what you're doing."

Naomi could feel her jaw slacken, and she had to wonder where her sister had picked up all this wisdom. She was smarter than all of them, and her mother said not a word.

"You know with Jerry and Chris, you and Daddy insisted they show up for Sunday dinner. Well, I for one would like to meet Cameron, and wouldn't it be really nice if he came for Sunday dinner so we could all talk like the civilized people we're supposed to be and get to know him and he us? Maybe then everyone would stop all this fighting and carrying on and having to walk on eggshells."

Naomi wanted to run up the steps and hug and kiss her sister. God, she loved her so much right now.

For the first time in days, her mother actually smiled. "Fine. You heard your sister, Naomi. Bring your Cameron by for Sunday dinner, and we'll talk like civilized people. Now you get to school," she said.

As Mason pulled open the screen door and her mother turned away, Naomi mouthed a thank-you to her, and Mason offered a conspiratorial wink. She was so touched by her younger sister, the baby, the only one in the family who hadn't treated her as if she didn't know what she was doing and was one big screw-up.

Chapter Twenty-Six

She was in his kitchen, reading a recipe and reaching up to tie back her long hair. He could tell by the weight of it that it really wasn't manageable but more something that was a part of her, that made up who she was. Maybe that was why he couldn't stop himself from touching her. Her hair, he loved running his hands over it, through it, and holding her to him while he kissed her, tasted her. He couldn't get the idea of her on her knees before him out of his mind, her long tresses fisted in his hand as he held her there. It was a thought that nearly brought him to his knees, but it was something that couldn't happen yet. He couldn't push, he couldn't rush. Naomi was the kind of girl he needed to give time, and then he would have her, all of her.

"So what are you making?" he asked as he slipped his hands in her hair before she could finish tying it back, lifting the long length, the dark brown that worked so much better on her than dyed blond.

"Moussaka, a Greek casserole, and you should know I've never made it before." She was so damn sweet, the way she glanced up at him, and he couldn't resist kissing her nose and lifting her glasses, then pressing a kiss to her lips, long and deep, his hands in her hair, holding her to him as he took what he was beginning to believe was his. He wanted all of her and had to make himself pull back. He had to make himself stop before he lifted her in his arms and took her to bed before she was ready.

"Your hair is like nothing I've seen before. It's so gorgeous and long, it seems as if you've never cut it," he said, taking in her sensitivity and quietness.

"I've always had long hair. I just let it grow as a child, and before long it became who I was. When my mom tried to cut it, I refused, and she learned after a while to respect that. Trims only. It's a lot to look after, too. I've thought of cutting it shorter a time or two recently, to something more manageable, but I haven't yet. I guess I'm not ready."

"Don't cut it. I like it. It's a guy thing to be able to have something to hold," he said, wondering how she'd respond. Maybe he wanted to see if she got it.

It was in her face, the way her eyes flickered, the heat that had him leaning in and kissing her again, deeper, as he leaned against the counter and fitted her between his legs, his hands slipping in her hair and then down and over the cotton of her pink tank top, over her curvy ass, fitted in relaxed cotton jeans. She rose on her tiptoes, her feet bare.

He needed to stop, as he was drowning, and in about two seconds he'd have her naked on this counter, driving into her. "Naomi, whoa…" he said when she slid her hands over his cheeks and tried to pull him down and kiss him again. "I'm going to have you stripped naked in a second. Slow it down now or I won't want to stop," he said. He slid his hands over her hips, holding her away, as he could feel how snug his jeans were. He could tell by the blush that she'd figured it out.

"What if I don't want to slow down?" she said, and instead of moving away as he'd expected, she stepped closer, pressed closer, and sighed. Yeah, it was something he couldn't hide.

"Not a good idea right now, Naomi, or there'll be no dinner, and I don't think you're ready," he said to her.

She was shaking her head as if arguing, and then she rose on her tiptoes, pressing her breasts and every soft part of her against all of his hardness, her lips pulling him closer, and she kissed him. "I'm ready, more ready than you know."

It was a second, maybe, and then he didn't think as he lifted her. She looped her arms around his neck, and Cameron, running on pure instinct and wanting this woman so badly, started down the wide open hallway to the master suite at the end of the hall. He settled her on his king-size bed and then stepped back a moment to take in the image. Yeah, she was perfect, and he couldn't wait to make her his.

HE WAS extraordinary as he pulled off his shirt, his chest and abs a work of art, and his shoulders appeared as if he could and had carried the weight of the world. "Take off your clothes," he said as he undid his belt, and she went up on her knees, pulling off her shirt and bra, taking in the heat in his eyes as he moved forward to her.

His hands ran over her breasts as he moved her back on the bed, running over the roundness that fit into his large hands just nicely. His hands trailed over her stomach, and he unsnapped her jeans and then pulled them off, leaving her in her black lace underwear. He pressed a kiss to her abdomen and lifted his head to see her reaction. It was all she could do to stay on the bed as he pressed her thighs wide, taking her in as if he were burning every inch of her to memory. Then he stepped back and out of his jeans, and he pulled off her underwear, his thumbs running over her thighs. He moved inside her, and the world as she knew it had never felt so right.

Chapter Twenty-Seven

It was something women referred to, or maybe it was men—she couldn't remember which in this moment. She was sated and complete, everything feeling so right, as if all the stars had aligned or something, as she laid against Cameron. He was a hard wall of muscle, and the circle of his arms was a perfect pillow.

The last time, he'd pulled her astride him and let her ride him while his hands guided her, played with her breasts, and touched every inch of her before she cried out his name and fell on top of him, and he'd held her tight for a moment. His hand now was drawing circles on her back, her leg tossed over his, and every bone in her body had turned to a limp noodle. She couldn't walk if she wanted to, and if she died right now she'd be a happy woman. She pressed a kiss to his chest.

"You're not like any woman I've ever known," he said after clearing his throat.

"In a good way, I hope?"

The rumble of laughter in his chest had her resting her chin on her hand, feeling his breath as she stared up at him. "You have no idea," he said, and then he turned serious, his large hand over her back, sliding down over her ass, squeezing a bit. She didn't think she could ever tire from his touch.

"Tell me about you, your family," she said. Other than what she knew plastered on the front page.

"Not much to tell. I have a father in Maine, divorced from my mother, Lori. Lori was an odd sort, I guess you can say. I never saw it, as I knew I was always her favorite. Dean was not. Thinking back now on everything, I can see how I allowed her to just take and do things. My father never did, and they fought something awful. I blamed him, thinking it was his fault for the breakup of our family, but it was him not allowing her childish ways and not taking any shit from her. I believed she'd been wronged when it was the other way around. I guess what I didn't see too is that Kari was just like her," he said, and she took a minute to realize who he was talking about.

"Your ex, the one who said all those horrible things about you in the press."

He lifted his hand to her cheek, and she leaned in. "And to anyone who would listen," he said. "You know it wasn't until this year that I let things go. It was easier to forgive my father, who I swore I never would, than it was for me to forgive the woman who was our mother, who took everything and tried to ruin me."

"Let me do a story on you that tells the truth about her, both of them, what they did to you…"

"No." He turned away and moved to the side of the bed, his feet over the edge, and she had to sit up. She needed to convince him, but he was shaking his head, and she could see how it completely set him on edge. "No, I said it before. That's not what this is, is it? Come in here, sleep with me, and then write a story?" He was accusing and getting louder, and she pulled the sheet up, trying to hide herself, feeling the anger and hurt, everything pummeling at her as if he suddenly saw her as the enemy.

"No, Cameron, I wouldn't do that. I just want everyone to see who you are, the real you, and to know the truth," she said.

He was now off the bed, pacing. His body was amazing, his thighs muscled, strong. "And I told you to drop it. Absolutely not. I don't want any more written about me. Don't you get it? All people will see is another headline, another story, and they'll put their own spin on it. It will blow up in my face. Not yours, not your life. Mine. No fucking way, Naomi, do I want to have my name whispered in the homes of every person I know and those I don't. The looks, the doors slammed, the problems. No more, Naomi. I lived through it, the gossip, and I'll never go through that again."

How could she get him to understand how important it was? "It would make a difference for my family, the truth."

The look he gave to her let her know that had been exactly the wrong thing to say.

"Hey, Cam?" someone called from the front. Then the door slammed, and the male voice and heavy footsteps had alarm bells shooting through her.

"Shit, Dean's here," Cameron said. He reached for his jeans, and Naomi pulled the sheet around her just as Dean stopped in the open doorway. His eyes widened, and she couldn't help the shriek that popped out of her. The timing was horrible.

"Oh, geez, so sorry. I didn't know. I'll wait..." He gestured and moved away as Cameron pulled on his clothes, strode over, and closed the door on him.

He turned back to her then. Everything loving in his face was gone. "If your family can't accept me without me having to turn my life upside down and expose myself for a story, then this will never work, because as much as I want you, I won't be plastered everywhere and have my life dissected under a microscope ever again." He pulled open the door, and she knew he was going to leave her.

"Cameron, I, uh… I just want something easy," she said, not knowing how to fix it.

The sad smile he sent her held a distance she didn't like. "Well, if you're looking for easy, that's not me and never will be," he said and stepped out of the bedroom, leaving her alone with her thoughts and her clothes strewn everywhere. She didn't know where this left them.

Chapter Twenty-Eight

Working her column wasn't exactly as bad as she'd thought it was going to be. In fact, she was enjoying writing community pieces, which were far more interesting than she'd expected. Although in her mind this wasn't real news reporting, it was still something, and it didn't bore her to tears.

It had been five days since she'd left Cameron's. He'd said a cold and distant goodbye after walking her to the door. Dinner had been forgotten, and so had the invitation to her parents' for Sunday. She'd had a long drive ahead of her, which had given her time to relive her thoughtless remark. How could she have said the story mattered to her family, as if doing it would have guaranteed her parents accepting him? Hindsight. She hated that word at times as she stared at her blank screen in her cubicle, hearing the buzzing of the newspaper office around her.

"Hey, you got a second?"

She jumped at the voice and turned to see Dean standing there. He was such a contrast to his brother, dark and hard, not oozing the same sort of chemistry that had her thinking of Cameron every waking moment. "Sure. How did you find me?" She looked around and wondered how he'd made his way this far back into the office, as well.

"Cameron told me where you worked. Wondered if you have a second to talk. Want to grab a coffee?" he asked, and she swallowed.

"Sure. There's a place downstairs," she said and opened her bottom drawer to pull out her purse, then stood and stuck her head around the corner to let Flory's assistant know, though the woman glanced up from her typing for only a moment.

Dean gestured for her to lead, and they weaved through the newsroom and out to the elevators, where he jabbed the button for down. She realized how tall he was, built like a boxer, a fighter. "Wanted to have a talk with you about my brother," he said.

What could she say, no? She wanted nothing more than to know how Cameron was, considering her heart ached at what she'd carelessly tossed out with her mouth. "Okay, how is he?" she asked as the elevator door opened. Two men inside were dressed in suits, heads down, texting on their phones. She stepped in, and Dean followed. The button for the lobby was already lit up.

"He's been better, which is why I'm here," he said.

The elevator slowed to the lobby, and the doors slid open. She stepped out, and Dean followed, walking across the mezzanine. Her slight heels echoed, and she was cool from the air conditioning in her black capris and silky blue top.

"I'm sorry to hear that. I kind of screwed up," she said, glancing over. There was nothing to say yes or no on his face. Boy, could this man hold his cards close to his chest.

"Yeah, but he may have overreacted. I told him that, and yes, I know how you wanted to do a story. It's kind of sweet, really, wanting to clear his name, but I don't think you understand how it burned him and pulled the rug right from under him. Unlike others, he doesn't curl up when he's hurt; he digs in and works hard and makes money, giving everything to his business, and he becomes a bitter, unforgiving asshole."

She wasn't sure what Dean was trying to say, so she stopped and looked up at him. This time he smiled and gestured with his chin to where Cameron was sitting at a table outside the cafe, talking on his cell phone. Her heart jumped, and she was frozen for a moment.

"He doesn't know I slipped upstairs to see you. Right now you have a choice: Walk away and go back to work and forget you saw him, and you're done for good. But Cameron, for the first time ever, was happy, and even though what you did, showing up at the bar to investigate him, totally pissed me off, I think you're good for him. So what will you do, Naomi?" He left it hanging, and she knew in that moment she could choose only one thing.

She reached out and touched Dean's arm. "Thank you," she said and started walking to where Cameron was. He hung up his phone and then looked around until his gaze connected with her as she approached and stopped right in front of him.

"Forgive me," she said. *For everything,* she willed him as she stood in front of him, aching over what she'd said, hoping he could let it go. *Please!*

His eyes were questioning, and he glanced around her.

"I only wanted to do something to fix some of the hurt you went through. My family…I shouldn't have said that, as it doesn't matter, and it wouldn't matter."

Then he stood up, so close to her that she had to look up at him. "But your family matters. They should matter," he said.

She didn't know if he'd leave or stay or what he meant. She nodded. "They do, I love them, and they'll just have to get to know you like I have. And when they do, they will accept you." Even if they didn't, she wouldn't walk away from him.

He slid his hand around her and pulled her closer, and her hands slid over his chest as she gazed up at him.

"Will you forgive me? Will you give me another chance?" she said, and this time his smile happened so slowly.

"Oh, I will, at that," he said before he leaned down and his lips touched hers. Cameron pulled her closer, kissing her deeply, his hand on her ass, and she didn't really care who was watching, because right now she was in the arms of the only man she wanted.

Turn the page for a sneak peek of
*WHAT WE CAN'T HAVE the next book in THE PARKER
SISTERS*
Available in print, Audio and eBook.

WHAT WE CAN'T HAVE

It all started the moment he laid eyes on me.

"You will cheer Mason on for her backbone and finally breaking free of the emotional chains of the family." Bookzilla

Love triangles can be complicated…especially when the heartthrob is a rodeo hero and two sisters end up vying to capture his heart!

CHAPTER 1

Scarlett had been making a damn fool of herself for the past half hour. It was embarrassing, the way she had every red-blooded American male staring her way—correction, their way, since Mason was seated beside her sister on the wooden bench in the covered arena where a cowboy on a bronc had just beaten the record time. She was whistling and yelling, making a spectacle that had every man drooling over how little she was wearing. Her shorts and silky tank with spaghetti straps barely covered her curves and charms. Her dark hair, now past her shoulders, was swept up in a sexy messy bun, making her look more like a beauty queen.

Mason had watched as hot cowboys climbed into the chute on top of one of the crazed horses, each time a different one. These macho cowboys who had come for the competition had more brass than brains, as far as she was concerned. Many of the men were locals, some from the surrounding area, with a few known and unknown additions from other states, all bad boys with no ambition, living for the rodeo and nothing else, the type of guys her father wouldn't have allowed within one hundred feet of his daughters.

It was easy to see how each of these cowboys lived for this life and the competition, only most would be thrown in seconds from the twisting ball of fire that had only one objective: to unseat the rider from its back. There were bone-jarring thuds, cracks, men flying in the air as if ragdolls before hitting the dirt, rolling on the ground in the split second they had to get out of the way of those crazed horses and their thousands of pounds of flesh and hooves that could come slamming into the ground just inches from the heads of cowboys who didn't move quick enough or weren't snatched out of the way by the rodeo clowns. Mason watched in horror, knowing that split second could cost a cowboy everything, even his life, or just break every bone in his body and end his career in a sport that was only for the young. To make it worse each time, she found herself holding her breath, waiting for the cowboy to move, waiting to see if he was okay. She was a damn wreck.

She'd watched each of those macho cowboys, some limping, some jogging away as if this were just another day, some shaking it off, some moving slower than others before climbing out of the ring. She stared, taking in the blood-thirsty sport. She knew each and every one of them would be stiff and sore and bruised from the suicidal ride that had lasted only seconds. She just didn't get what it was that made these guys want to risk their lives. Did they want to win the purse, the prize? It was just a buckle, a pittance, nothing that could come close in any way to balancing the scales. That was the question that continued to plague her as she sat on the uncomfortable bench: What possessed those guys to risk everything for nothing?

It was all in the hands of fate and came down to the draw. Not one of them knew until moments before which horse he would ride. Would it be one that gave him the edge or would it be an animal from hell? Mason sat tensely on the bench, furious at Scarlett for dragging her along, as she watched the latest cowboy lift his hand as he climbed over the rail. Another one done, so she could breathe a little easier for a second as they waited for the next guy to be called for his turn.

"Mason," Scarlett said as she took her seat again. The man seated behind her, who had stared at the way she wouldn't keep her butt planted on that wooden bench, was either disappointed or pleased. Mason thought it was the former, considering her jumping and cheering had given him a better view of her butt cheeks, which were showing from under her too-short shorts. If her parents had any idea where they were and how Scarlett was dressed and carrying on, she and Mason would both be in some serious hot water. "You look as if you're going to pass out," Scarlett said. "What is wrong with you? Get up, have some fun."

Yeah, she was seriously going to kill her sister. "Oh, I don't know. How about the fact that we're watching grown men hop on the back of some devil hell bent on killing them for the chance to, what, either break their necks or win some buckle they can show off for years, bragging about how they held on for eight seconds and lived to tell the tale?" She allowed the sarcasm to flow, knowing no one in her family had any idea how much she disliked bronc riding. She found it cruel to both the horse and rider. It was the one event she wished they'd ban. But here was her sister, carrying on like a fool, grabbing her and shaking her, the biggest supporter of this bloodthirsty sport.

"This is so exciting. He's next," Scarlett hissed, and her

fingers wrapped around Mason's wrist, digging in a little too hard. It was her latest crush, the cowboy she'd been talking about nonstop for weeks, Justin Broadstone. "Get ready for a seriously drool-worthy cowboy," she said. "I'm not kidding you. I swear wranglers were created for this man. Wait until you see him. Man candy, got to have him. This guy has it all."

Mason cringed, knowing everyone could hear how Scarlett had ogled someone so indecently. For a minute, she wished there was an empty seat beside her—or, even better, two rows back—so she could move, but there wasn't, as the arena was full, everyone going crazy for this ridiculous event. They were all insane. She heard the announcer call his name, and the crowd went wild. Her sister was screaming, jumping again, her breasts bouncing under that tank without a bra. Scarlett had seriously lost her mind.

Mason was so done. Just one more ride, and then she'd drag her sister out of there before she did or said something that got both of them into an even more embarrassing situation—and before she could cause any trouble that would get back to her parents. Mason knew she would get tarred with the same brush. Fortunately, everyone was standing now for the crowd favorite, which helped her to hide, giving her a moment of anonymity, considering they were in the front row, way too close and in the open.

Women were going crazy. Scarlett reached down and yanked Mason by the arm to pull her up from the spot where she was hunkered down, trying to stay hidden. She could see the cowboy, tall, dark hair. Scarlett hadn't lied: The man was seriously hot as he jogged to the ring, climbed over the rails, and took his seat on the crazed horse, which was already bouncing and snorting. He settled a black cowboy hat on his head. His short dark hair was just a little wavy, and she was struck by how broad his shoulders were. That seemed to set him apart from every other hot cowboy out there. Maybe that was what unsettled her as she watched his focus, his determination. He completely rattled her.

The crowd went crazy when the horse leaped and crashed against the rail. The hot cowboy jumped, and his long legs moved fast. He grasped the rungs of the rail before his leg could be crushed. The team of cowboys was there beside him, settling the horse and getting him ready again, and Mason couldn't take her eyes off the scene. The black horse seemed to have been spawned by the devil himself, snorting and out for blood. Buckle bunnies were screaming the rider's name on the other side of the arena, bouncing, having lost every basic shred of decency, hell bent on getting that cowboy to know they existed: "Justin, I love you!" "Justin, I want you!" "Ride that horse and you can ride me next!"

Mason was horrified at the boldness and the blatant sexually descriptive cackling. Her jaw dropped. These women had no shame, and she was embarrassed for them, for him. Justin didn't seem to notice, which was a wonder, considering one busty woman had a neon pink sign that read, *Justin, I'm going to marry you.* Some women two rows back, who had been quiet until now, were now screaming out how they were going to suck his cock and wanted to have his babies. Mason wasn't sure what strangled sound came from her throat.

Then he looked right at her.

In that moment in time, she wished the ground would open up and swallow her whole, because she realized he was looking at her as if she'd said those words, making her feel as if she'd tossed herself naked his way. This was worse than she could have imagined.

He still hadn't looked away. His face was amazing: hard, chiseled, with a square jaw and eyes that seemed to connect just with her, as if it were just her and him. Then he turned away and nodded to one of the cowboys, who pressed his gloved hand to his shoulder as the horn blasted and the chute opened.

Everyone was up on their feet. Mason watched in horror as the seconds ticked by, as if everything were resting on that clock. For a moment she saw things in slow motion as the sounds around her drowned and were muffled. By the way the rider hung on and gripped that rope, it was as if he and that horse from hell were one. Then the buzzer sounded. Justin jumped off the horse, and the crowd went wild as he leaped up onto the rail with a killer smile, dimples flashing. His eyes again landed on her.

"He's looking this way," Scarlett hissed. Then she was screaming again, calling his name. She was crazed, jumping just like all the other women who were vying for his attention.

Mason had finally had enough, but she spotted him jumping down from the rail, landing in the dirt, and now walking their way. Her stomach bottomed out. The fans were going crazy. Her legs bolted her upright suddenly, as if they had a mind of their own. She was done.

"We're leaving now!" she hissed to Scarlett, then grabbed her wrist and pulled hard, putting everything into dragging her sister out of there, elbowing the people beside her as she tried to step around them while they cheered and clapped. Scarlett was hitting her arm, her hand, trying to break the grip as Mason dragged her out to the aisle, to the concrete steps, up the stairs.

"Mason, let go of me right now! What the hell are you doing? Stop!" Scarlett demanded as Mason saw the exit sign just ahead. Almost there, and then she'd shove Scarlett into the used pickup her sister Taz had given to her. Considering she lived in Denver now with her new husband, Jerry, a man who could give her the world, Taz no longer had need of it. Mason had thanked her, a kind sister who was sane and would never throw herself so shamefully at a man.

Five more steps. She could hear the announcer calling the time, saying something else, and the crowd was still going crazy. She stopped listening, as her sister was digging in her heels, but Mason was stronger, more determined. The crowd was going wild behind her again. What the hell?

There was security by the door, two men, and they were looking at her as if she were the one who'd lost her mind. It seemed as if they were blocking her way. Then a big hand touched her arm.

"Hey," said someone with a deep voice that had her heart taking a nosedive.

Her nerves were so frazzled that she jumped and turned. Seeing the shock on Scarlett's face alone was priceless, and Mason was positive her jaw dropped as she looked up at the cowboy who had just gone the distance, Justin Broadstone. He was standing in front of her and Scarlett, but he was looking straight at her—unsettling, insane. It was a second or less, but it seemed like an eternity, a moment in time that could have been just her and him. What the hell? For the first time today, Scarlett was silent.

"What the…" She stopped and knew everyone had their eyes on him and her. She hated being the center of attention. There may as well have been a spotlight shining their way, because everyone was watching them, listening to everything they had to say. The door was right there.

"Who are you?" Justin asked.

Scarlett bumped shoulders with her, and she nearly lost

her footing. The cowboy's hand went up, touching her shoulder. Zap! The jolt from his large warm hand was beyond what she could have expected.

"I'm Scarlett Parker," Scarlett said. "Justin, I just absolutely loved your ride. You're so amazing. I just love watching you out there, the way you do everything so perfectly. So amazing. There's no one better, and…"

Oh my good God. Mason was horrified, embarrassed at how her sister was drooling over this man, yet he was giving her no attention. In fact, he glanced Scarlett's way only a second, but it was as if he'd heard nothing. Then he gave everything to Mason once again, all of his attention.

And damn, his eyes, which she could see close up now, were whiskey colored, amber, lit with a fire she'd never seen before. It was deep and intense, and for a moment he made her feel as if he was looking so deep inside her that he could see every inch of her body, her skin, naked in front of him.

"Your name, what is your name?" he asked her again. This time he stepped closer. She could feel his heat, and it was just her and him. There was nobody getting in between them.

"Mason Parker," she said, her throat thick.

She heard her sister hiss beside her as the cowboy nodded. He was taking over her space, stopping her from stepping one more foot out that door, as if she were the only person who existed right now. He offered her a crooked smile that reached his eyes, and it was like dynamite. The power and electricity that connected them left her limp and unable to take another step.

"Mason, I'm Justin. That ride was for you," he said, taking his black cowboy hat from his head and setting it on hers before he was pulled away by the other cowboys she hadn't seen standing there. He needed to be back in the arena to get his buckle and prize and whatever else, because he was the winner. She stared after him in horror, feeling the heat of the hat on her head and then taking in Scarlett, who was staring at her as if she'd done the one thing she'd never do: betray her.

About the Author

"Lorhainne Eckhart is one of my go to authors when I want a guaranteed good book. So many twists and turns, but also so much love and such a strong sense of family."

(Lora W., Reviewer)

New York Times & USA Today bestseller Lorhainne Eckhart is best known for her writing Raw Relatable Real Romances, where "Morals and family are running themes. Danger, romance, and a drive to do what is right will see you glued to the page." As one fan calls her, she is the "Queen of the family saga." (aherman) writing "the ups and downs of what goes on within a family but also with some suspense, angst and of course a bit of romance thrown in for good measure." Follow Lorhainne on Bookbub to receive alerts on New Releases and Sales and join her mailing list at LorhainneEckhart.com for her Monday Blog, books news, giveaways and FREE reads. With over 120 books, audiobooks, and multiple series published and available at all retailers now translated into six languages. She is a multiple recipient of the Readers' Favorite Award for Suspense and Romance, and lives in the Pacific Northwest on an island, is the mother of three, her oldest has autism and she is an advocate for never giving up on your dreams.

"Lorhainne Eckhart has this uncanny way of just hitting the spot every time with her books."

(Caroline L., Reviewer)

The O'Connells: *The O'Connells of Livingston, Montana are not your typical family. A riveting collection of stories surrounding the ups and downs of what goes on within a family but also with some suspense, angst and of course a bit of romance thrown in for good measure "I thought I loved the Friessens, but I absolutely adore the O'Connell's. Each and every book has totally different genres of stories but the one thing in common is how she is able to wrap it around the family which is the heart of each story." (C. Logue)*

The Friessens: *An emotional big family romance series, the Friessen family siblings find their relationships tested, lay their hearts on the line, and discover lasting love! "Lorhainne Eckhart is one of my go to authors when I want a guaranteed good book. So many twists and turns, but also so much love and such a strong sense of family." (Lora W., Reviewer)*

The Parker Sisters: *The Parker Sisters are a close-knit family, and like any other family they have their ups and downs. "Eckhart has crafted another intense family drama…The character development is outstanding, and the emotional investment is high…" (Aherman, Reviewer)*

The McCabe Brothers: *Join the five McCabe siblings on their journeys to the dark and dangerous side of love! An intense, exhilarating collection of romantic thrillers you won't want to miss. — "Eckhart has a new series that is definitely worth the read. The queen of the family saga started this series with a spin-off of her wildly successful Friessen series." From a Readers' Favorite award—winning author and "queen of the family saga" (Aherman)*

Billy Jo McCabe Mystery: *The social worker and the cop, an unlikely couple drawn together on a small, secluded Pacific Northwest island where nothing is as it seems. Protecting the innocent comes at a cost, and what seems to be a sleepy, quiet town is anything but.*

Lorhainne loves to hear from her readers! You can connect with me at:
www.LorhainneEckhart.com
lorhainneeckhart.le@gmail.com

facebook.com/AuthorLorhainneEckhart

twitter.com/LEckhart

instagram.com/lorhainneeckhart

bookbub.com/profile/lorhainne-eckhart

pinterest.com/lorhainneeckhart

In the Family
In the Silence
In the Charm
Unexpected Consequences
It Was Always You
The First Time I Saw You
Welcome to My Arms
Welcome to Boston
I'll Always Love You
Ground Rules
A Reason to Breathe
You Are My Everything
Anything For You
The Homecoming
Stay Away From My Daughter
The Bad Boy
A Place of Our Own
The Visitor
All About Devon
Long Past Dawn
How to Heal a Heart
Keep Me In Your Heart

The O'Connells
The Neighbor
The Third Call
The Secret Husband
The Quiet Day
The Commitment
The Missing Father
The Hometown Hero
Justice
The Family Secret

The Fallen O'Connell
The Return of the O'Connells
And The She Was Gone
The Stalker
The O'Connell Family Christmas
The Girl Next Door

The McCabe Brothers
Don't Stop Me (Vic)
Don't Catch Me (Chase)
Don't Run From Me (Aaron)
Don't Hide From Me (Luc)
Don't Leave Me (Claudia)
Out of Time

A Billy Jo McCabe Mystery
Nothing As it Seems
Hiding in Plain Sight
The Cold Case
The Trap
Above the Law

The Wilde Brothers
The One (Joe and Margaret)
The Honeymoon, A Wilde Brothers Short
Friendly Fire (Logan and Julia)
Not Quite Married, A Wilde Brothers Short
A Matter of Trust (Ben and Carrie)
The Reckoning, A Wilde Brothers Christmas
Traded (Jake)
Unforgiven (Samuel)
The Holiday Bride

Married in Montana
His Promise
Love's Promise
A Promise of Forever

The Parker Sisters
Thrill of the Chase
The Dating Game
Play Hard to Get
What We Can't Have
Go Your Own Way
A June Wedding

Kate & Walker
One Night
Edge of Night
Last Night

Walk the Right Road Series
The Choice
Lost and Found
Merkaba
Bounty
Blown Away: The Final Chapter

The Saved Series
Saved
Vanished
Captured

Single Titles
He Came Back
Loving Christine

For my German Readers
Die Außenseiter-Reihe
Der Vergessene Junge
Der Gefallene Held

For my French Readers
L'ENFANT OUBLIÉ